TINSEY CLOVER

Chelsea Walker Flagg

Published and Printed in the United States

ISBN 978-0-9967284-9-2 (trade paper)
ISBN 978-0-9967284-8-5 (ebook)

Cover Design by Kelly Angelovic
Book Formatting by Polgarus Studio

Dedicated to my three
adventurous and brave daughters:
Quincy, Olive, and Pearl

CHAPTER ONE

Today's the day. The day I'm finally going to sneak out of Snugglepunk to explore the rest of the Bungaborg Forest. Of course, I said the same thing yesterday. And the day before. And the day before that. But, today, I really mean it.

I brush a strand of shaggy purple hair out of my full moon emerald green eyes and make a thirty-degree turn to the right followed by forty-four paces. A full right-angle turn to the left then another hundred-and-seven steps. I calculate the path with precision, quietly weaving my way in and out of massive brown tree trunks so old, you could climb into their wrinkles and stay hidden for weeks. The trees shoot up most likely all the way to space, spreading their enormous, greedy branches to hog all the sunlight for themselves.

Not to brag or anything, but I'm pretty much an expert sneaker. I mean, when you've done something as much as I've done this, it's hard not to be an expert. Another ninety degree right turn. I'm close now. Thirty more yards, which is no small distance when you're only the size of a chipmunk. Still, my bare feet know the way by heart. They glide quickly over the mossy ground beneath me.

I tune into my slightly pointy ears for a second. Part of being a great sneaker is using all your senses. I hear the call of the morning Icelandic birds and a soft, melodic humming of the other trealfur elves waking up. It's not an unusual sound. Trealfur elves always hum. It's just something you do when you've got the best singing voices in the forest.

I never hum. Because, unlike every other trealfur elf in Snugglepunk, my voice does not sound like chimes tingling on a soft breeze. No way. I'm pretty sure a better comparison would be to say my voice sounds like an angry honey badger with a head cold. Who's also dying. That about sums it up.

In front of me, a solid vine wall comes into view. The twenty foot wall my grandpa built before I was born that wraps all the way around the perimeter to keep Snugglepunk safe from the rest of the Bungaborg Forest. The border that's always made me feel trapped.

Last year, when I was only ten, I found a good size hole in the vines. Approximately twelve inches by five inches I'd say, which would be just big enough for an elf my size to slip through without too much trouble. Guess how many times I've thought about doing just that? That's right. A lot. I run the remaining few feet and stop at the looming wall.

I press my copper hands against the thick vines and stand on my toes, the tip of my tongue pushing out of the corner of my mouth like it always does when I'm concentrating on something. I close one eye and take a peek. Even though I've seen this view at least a hundred times now, it still sends chills right down my spine. It's the only exposure I've ever had to the outside world.

I know from my lessons that the Bungaborg

Forest is set up in a faery ring, which is exactly what it sounds like: a thick of trees that makes the shape of a giant ring. All the different forest people, or Huldufolk, live in separate villages spaced out within the wooded ring. In the center of the ring is a wide-open meadow, or the engi. No one lives there. At least no one with half a brain. It's far too dangerous and exposed for anyone to survive out there. Or so everyone says. But, dangerous or not, the engi is pretty awesome looking.

I push myself even higher on my tiptoes and try to see as much as I can. The little rays of morning sunlight are firing everything up and turning the engi into a vast, golden space. In the far distance, I can just barely see the other side of the faery ring. I shift my gaze fifteen degrees to the right and gasp. There it is. Plethora, the blomalfur elfin town. At least I'm pretty sure it's Plethora. The trees are spaced in exact increments and I swear, especially at this time of day, I can even see perfectly-placed sparkles glowing in the trees.

From what I've heard, the blomalfur elves love beauty and math. Why wouldn't they intentionally space their trees and add something glittery to make their village shine? I'm pretty sure there was a mistake when I was born. I was supposed to be a blomalfur elf, not a trealfur elf. That's why today's the day I'm gonna sneak out of here.

"Hey, dork, your tongue's sticking out again," my brother's voice taunts me from behind.

It gives me just enough of a startle to lose my concentration. And my balance. I topple forward into the vine wall, bounce off, and land face up on the mossy ground. I scramble to my feet and brush my clothes off. Not that it matters much. Trealfurs aren't known for their sense of fashion. We use rabbit hair to stitch together dull bits of soft tree bark and dying leaves, and call it an outfit. Boring, right?

Leaves more creativity and time to focus on our music, Mom always says, even though I don't see why we can't be efficient and fashionable all at once.

"You're a punk," I scold my brother, a chunk of my purple hair flopping itself right over my eyes. "You can't just come up and scare me like that."

How did he follow me here without me noticing? So much for thinking I'm such a great sneaker.

"Serves you right," Aspen teases with a shake of his head.

Even with the movement, his icy blue hair sits annoyingly still on his golden forehead. It wouldn't dare venture down to his eyes like mine does, because like everything else about Aspen, his hair is perfect. I resist the urge to reach out and tussle it.

"You're the one who's always spying on the blomalfurs," Aspen says. "I mean, what's so great about them anyway? They're elves just like us."

"They're geniuses," I correct. "I bet they even think in numbers. I want to be just like them when I grow up."

"Yeah, well that's never gonna happen," Aspen shrugs. "You're a trealfur, not a blomalfur. Besides, you're not supposed to be here. Mom and Dad would be livid if they knew you spent all your time peeking out of this little hole so close to the engi."

Aspen used to be fun. Like, really fun. We used

to skip out on our chores all the time to run around Snugglepunk. We'd pretend we were explorers on dangerous expeditions, or sometimes pirates searching for lost treasure. Not anymore, though. Ever since his thirteenth birthday, Aspen's been acting more and more like a stodgy old grown-up. In other words, he's become Boring with a capital B.

"I should totally tell on you," he says.

I shake my head so hard, it makes me dizzy. I do not need my parents, or even worse, my uncle, to know I'm here. Even though he's a punk, Aspen lets the topic go.

"Anyway," he changes the subject, "we've gotta go. Uncle Vondur's called an emergency council meeting. Another fire just broke out at the other edge of Snugglepunk, the second one this week! Still no idea who keeps starting these things. This is getting pretty serious, Tins. Mom asked me to come and find you."

CHAPTER TWO

Council meetings are the worst. Talk about Boring with a capital B. Not all the kids in Snugglepunk have to go to them, but when your mother is the sister of the King and his only heir, you're expected to attend humdrum events like council meetings.

Aspen's walking away from me, and as much as I'd rather stay right here and try to count the glitter in the Plethora trees, I know I need to go with him. He starts chanting a loud, strange yipping noise that sounds absolutely ridiculous. However, whatever he's doing is working because out of nowhere, a pair of sleek, arctic foxes sprint out of the trees, breaking through the last wisps of fog floating just over the ground. They stop right in front of Aspen. The animals tilt their heads from one side to the other, listening closely to his noises.

Finally, they nod their response.

"They said they'll take us so we can get there quicker," Aspen calls out. "C'mon!"

I'll never admit it out loud, but I will say, I feel a teensy bit jealous looking at those foxes. Aspen's ability to communicate with animals popped up on the exact morning he turned eleven. My birthday was three whole days ago, which technically makes me eleven-and-point-oh-oh-eight-years old, and my gift still hasn't shown up. I'm trying to be patient, but I can't wait to see what unique power I land. Maybe I'll be able to summon windstorms just by humming like Dad. Or what if I get something like Mom's power? When she sings above a certain pitch, the entire forest—huldufolk and animals alike—stops for a split second to listen. I'm not sure what good that will ever do her, but it's still pretty awesome.

What I'm really hoping for is the power to get out of Snugglepunk and go somewhere I won't get laughed at when my mind thinks in numbers, not music notes. Like Plethora. Of course I can be patient for something like that.

"Seriously, Tins, I'm gonna leave without you," Aspen breaks into my thoughts.

I huff extra loud to make sure he can hear me, then straighten my green duds and saunter into the woods. Very. Slowly. Sometimes it's necessary to act like a brat to your brother for no good reason.

"Your funeral, not mine," Aspen shrugs.

I speed up and scramble onto one of the fox's backs, feeling bad for tugging at its fur. It doesn't even seem to notice, though. That's both the joy, and the frustration, of being the size of a chipmunk. I could never make enough of a dent in things for it to matter much.

We speed through the forest, zig-zagging between tree trunks so huge not even a giant could wrap his arms around one, let alone find the radius and diameter on the thing. The morning fog's mostly gone now, which makes it much easier to see the little burst of reds and yellows from the wildflowers that grow here. The most colorful item around though is Aspen's hair. Although, I must say, it looks less like hair and much more like a blue blur as he races ahead of me on his fox.

Pretty soon, all the head honcho trealfurs come into view, sitting knee to knee to form an oval. At first, each of the trealfurs looks like a tiny ant, but they quickly grow as our foxes dart closer toward the council spot.

Aspen barks sharply, and his fox comes to a halt right away. Of course. My fox, on the other hand, doesn't even slow down, let alone stop. Maybe it didn't hear Aspen's orders, but I know better. This fox is just being cheeky, because that's how wild animals are with me sometimes. It's like they know I don't fit in here, too. All I can do is hold on as my rowdy critter runs at full speed straight into the circle. Trealfurs scatter and roll everywhere, trying not to get run over. And still, my ride barrels forward. That's another thing about animals: they are not always sensible.

Tucking my chin to my chest, I let go and bounce off, hitting the cold green blanket of moss and leaves on the ground. I don't have much time to notice how it feels to have the air knocked out of my lungs before my whole body rolls noggin over knees and shoulders over shins. Funny sounds pop out of my mouth that I have absolutely no control over.

"Ooof! Eeef! Ouch!" And, my personal favorite: "AIEEEEE!"

I summersault straight toward Uncle Vondur, the King of the Bungaborg Trealfurs, forcing him to dive out of my way. But, I don't stop there. No sirree. I careen right past him and into a large bush. Some might think rolling into a bush is a lucky thing, and usually I would agree. Unless it happens to be a very healthy thistle plant. Don't get me wrong, the purple burrs on a thistle plant are quite beautiful, but just not so much when you're rolling around in them.

The second that plant latches onto me, it's clear it has no intention of ever letting go. It holds firmly onto my golden arms, my pointed ears, my freshly tangled purple locks. *At least it's keeping my hair out of my eyes*, I think, trying to stay positive. Mom would be proud of me for that.

Where is Mom anyway? I scan the circle, which is really more of a pile now. Mom's near the top of the stack of trealfurs, her light pink hair looking like a worn-out daddy long-leg spider on her head. She stares straight back at me with the same emerald eyes she gave me. I manage a little smile and mouth the word *oops*. Mom smiles back at me with a twinkle in her eyes, as if to say *it happens to the best of us*, even though I know it most certainly does not.

After an exhausting struggle, I finally free myself from the wrath of the thistles. Meanwhile, the pile of trealfurs has rearranged itself back into a wonky oval. I'm not sure why my people can't even make something as simple as an oval look right. Even still, they all look so put together, it's almost as if a wild animal hadn't just smashed through, playing bowling for trealfurs. Of course, the looks on everyone's faces suggest otherwise. Everyone's grumbling at me as though I just brought a falcon into the council meeting or something. Yeesh. Like I'd ever do anything that nasty.

Aspen takes a seat on the ground next to Dad, which leaves only one spot open for me. Right in between Mom and Uncle Vondur, aka King of the Trealfurs. Yikes. Talk about bad luck. That thistle bush suddenly doesn't seem like such a terrible place to be.

CHAPTER THREE

On one side of me, Mom's got a plastered-on smile, as if she's trying to pretend nothing out of the ordinary just happened. On the other side, Uncle Vondur's glaring straight at me. His thick, black eyebrows are scrunched into a disapproving V.

"I'm going to assume you'll punish Tinsey appropriately for so rudely disrupting our entire meeting," Uncle Vondur says, presumably to my parents even though he's still looking at me.

Mom nods without breaking her forced smile. "Sure thing."

"Very well then," Uncle Vondur growls. "Let's not waste any more time."

He turns his attention toward the whole group, then draws the wooden flute hanging around his neck up to his lips and begins to play a tune to indicate the start of the meeting. *Whew.* Getting stared down by the king of your people is not a great feeling. The king lowers the instrument then chants a string of notes. Everyone in the circle echoes him in perfect, glorious harmony. I open my mouth and pretend to chant along. Uncle Vondur gives me a stern look.

"Sing for real, Tinsey," Mom urges from next to me. "You're being disrespectful."

I swallow hard and let my voice rise from my throat. "LAAA!"

Everyone stops mid-note and stares at me, their mouths all still dropped open. Mom shakes her head. Uncle Vondur scowls. See what I mean? A dying honey badger with a head cold.

"Let's just move along, shall we?" The annoyance in Uncle Vondur's voice is loud and clear. "Welcome to Council," he booms, tossing back his black ponytail.

He always has a serious tone to his voice, but he really likes to lay it on thick when he's talking to his people.

"As always, let's all give praise to the Snugglepunk Safety Stone that keeps all the dangerous huldufolk out."

Uncle Vondur looks and points toward a spot high in the trees, where no such thing as a stone can be seen. Who knows if it even exists. Everyone lifts a hand and mumbles a mantra to the unseen gem.

"There's no time for formalities today now that we're running so far behind schedule," Uncle Clover says once the mumbling is done. He shoots another dirty look in my direction.

Yeesh, I think. *We get it already. You're not happy with me.*

"So, we'll have to skip straight to our most serious issue at hand."

All the heads in the circle nod. Everyone always agrees with King Vondur, no matter what. I shake my head side to side, just to switch things up a bit.

A little diversity is a good thing, right?

"As you all know, there's been yet another fire at the edge of Snugglepunk," the king says. "Just this morning."

Murmers roll through the group. Uncle Vondur puts his hands up and everyone stops talking immediately.

"I know, I know," he says. "We all have a lot of questions. First, let me say, everyone and everything is fine. Luckily, the fire was started right by the Bungaborg Pond again, so we were able to quickly extinguish the flames. We still don't have any leads to who's causing such destruction to our village…"

"It's got to be the yulemen!" one trealfur shouts out, interrupting the king. "Those cheeky buggers are always up to no good."

"No way," another council member chimes in. "If you ask me, it's definitely the sprites. I hear they don't have a single nice bone in their bodies."

"It's the trolls!" yet another voice. "Of course it's the trolls. Everyone knows trealfurs taste like candy to those brutes. They obviously want to smoke us out of our homes so they can eat us!"

The whole circle of trealfurs is riled up now, yelling over each other and trying to make their opinions heard. Uncle Vondur puts his hands up again. Just like that, the council falls silent.

"It's true, it could be any number of huldufolk responsible for these monstrosities," he agrees with everyone at once.

Leaders are supposed to be diplomatic like that, or so I hear.

I'm not sure anyone can say for sure who's starting these fires. I'm not even certain anyone here has ever even seen any of the other huldufolk, let alone gotten to know them well enough to say whether or not they're mean enough to set someone else's town ablaze.

The shouting and blaming starts to pick up again, turning into a rather loud din.

"Enough!" Uncle Vondur shouts, clearly losing his patience. "Quiet down, all of you!"

The circle falls silent. Everyone knows better than to cross the king.

"Quite frankly, it is of zero importance what everyone thinks about this situation. The only thing that matters is what we can do to track down the culprit, prove their guilt, and punish them to the utmost level of the law. To do that, I have decided to ask for rotating volunteers to monitor the area every hour of the day. Together, we'll get to the bottom of this."

My brain quickly does the math. One-hundred-and-ninety-two trealfurs in Snugglepunk divided by twenty-four hours in the day. Which means we'll each be watching this spot in our town for seven-and-a-half-minutes every day? What a drag. My mind drifts off yet again at his phrase: rotating volunteers. I can't help but picture a giant polar bear coming in from outside of the Bungaborg Forest to volunteer. It'd march back and forth across the edge of town. Only, every ninety-nine paces, it'd flip upside down and start using its legs to push itself and rub its white, furry back along the ground. Get it? It's rotating. I giggle at my own joke, but realize too late I'm not just laughing to myself. All eyes shift to me again.

"Do you think this is all a big game, Miss Clover?" Uncle Vondur booms.

I shake my head, but can't knock the smile off my face. Rotating bears volunteering to keep our forest safe. It's just too funny. I open my mouth to try to explain the image to everyone else. Dad lowers his head into his hand like he realizes what I'm about to say.

"I was just thinking..." I start, but cut myself off. How do I explain this? "I was picturing something in my mind," I say. But suddenly, the word bear disappears from my vocabulary. "I was thinking about a...um...a..." The word won't come.

I snap my fingers together, trying to drum it up. The word doesn't come back to me, but something else happens entirely. A broom appears in a puff of smoke and sparkles by my side from out of nowhere. I know, it sounds crazy, but that's really what happens. The wooden broom pops up and starts sweeping the ground next to me. What in the world? It nudges my knees, and I scoot backward to let it pass. It makes its way sweeping through the entire circle of trealfurs until the ground we've all been sitting on is spotless. Well, as spotless as a section of ground in the middle of an Icelandic forest can be. Once the cleaner's job is done, it disappears just as quickly as it came. We all sit in silence for a few seconds, mouths wide open in wonder.

I feel a little lightheaded and a tingling sensation runs up and down my spine as a growing suspicion sneaks into my thoughts. Could this actually be happening? I stand up on wobbly legs and snap my fingers again, just to test things out. Sure enough, a sudsy hallowed out tree-stump bucket falls from the sky and plops down next to me, the water sloshing all over the place. That thing would take weeks to make by hand. Trust me, I know.

The foreign bowl starts splashing some sort of lemon-smelling solution all over everyone's leaf clothing, making council members jump left and right in shock. After the thing targets the last trealfur, it disappears just like the broom.

"Uh…" Mom mutters from her spot in the circle, her shirt dripping wet. "Sweetheart?" She says to me in more of a question than a statement. "I believe you may be coming into your magic?"

CHAPTER FOUR

This is my gift? I'm so confused. And tired. Did I seriously just gain the ability to snap my fingers and summon cleaning tools into existence? What a crock. I mean, shouldn't I at least be allowed the gift to not sound like a really upset seal whenever I sing a note? I can't imagine anyone in the history of ever actually getting excited about my new, strange magic. I scan the circle and notice every single eye staring at me in utter awe. I take that back. Ninety-nine-point-nine percent of the trealfurs in this circle look in complete astonishment over this. Want to guess who makes up the point-oh-one percent of trealfurs who isn't getting a kick out of this whole situation? That's right: Me.

So, why am I the one who gained this bizarre

power? I glance around the circle again. Everyone's looking back at me like I just turned into a two-headed walrus or something. Two minutes ago, people were shooting daggers out of their eyes at me like I was the scum of the earth, and now, here they all are, acting like I'm the most amazing creature to ever walk the face of the planet.

"Do it again," one of the trealfurs urges in a loud whisper.

A few others nod their heads in enthusiastic agreement. It's clear they all want to see what other sparkly new cleaners I can make appear out of nowhere. I really don't want to test it out anymore, but a tiny voice inside my head wonders if maybe, just maybe, this "gift" is actually a fluke. I mean, I did hit my head pretty hard when I rolled off that fox. What if that knocked things loose a little bit? I cross one set of fingers behind my back and hope that'll work to help my wish come true, then close one eye before snapping my other set of fingers again. *Please just be a big mistake*, I think. Unfortunately, it's not. Another broom appears in a cloud of sparkles just like the last one, and falls to the ground with a clatter.

A round of applause ripples through the council circle. I bury my head in my hands.

How unlucky can one girl get?

My knees suddenly feel like wet blades of grass. I crumble to the ground in pure exhaustion.

Mom rushes to my side and cradles my heavy head in her hand. With her free hand, she scrounges through a fold in her dress and pulls out a small wooden vile.

"Here," she says softly, popping off the top of the bottle and pushing it toward my lips.

I take a sip. Lavender oil.

"It helps revive you after you use your power," Mom says.

I count the seconds in my head. Twenty-three, twenty-four. At exactly twenty-five seconds, I feel totally normal again and not a bit tired. Mom smiles, like she was counting the seconds in her head, too. She helps me to my feet and brushes me off.

"I must say," Uncle Vondur comes up to us from behind, his voice surprisingly gentle given what it sounded like just a few minutes ago. "You have impressed me here today, Tinsey. Nice work!"

He wraps a stiff arm around me in an awkward attempt at a side hug. Uncle Vondur's never been one for showing much affection, so I know this is a big deal. I try to smile up at him, but the corners of my mouth won't turn the right way. For the record, my uncle has the coolest gift ever. The guy can straight up fly. Seriously. When he turned eleven, he gained the ability to launch himself into the air. And yet, here he is impressed by my measly new talent to produce a bucket of soapy water from out of nowhere. Talk about unfair.

"That's my girl!" Dad chimes in from my other side, also wrapping an arm around me. He's much better at giving hugs. "I knew you'd get something really cool." He gently presses his fist onto my cheek and makes my whole neck tilt a little, the way adults do to kids when they're really proud of them.

That's when I notice Aspen. His blue hair is bobbing up and down on his head from silently laughing so hard. I can tell he's trying to stifle it, but he's doing a lousy job. What a punk. I squint my eyes down to little slits. Why does he get to talk to animals while I'm stuck imagining up brooms and buckets? I'll say it again: this is so not fair.

CHAPTER FIVE

"We're really proud of you, Tinsey," Mom says back in our family cave. "You're really coming into yourself."

Maybe I'm making it up, but her smile looks just as fake as it did back in the council circle.

I give a feeble smile back even though I feel much more frustrated than proud at the moment. I press my back against one of the rocky gray walls of the cave and slide down to a cross-legged position on the floor. Can't mom see how miserable this whole fiasco is making me?

"Why am I so different?" I blurt.

Mom's smile fades, leaving a straight-across mouth in its place. She walks over to me and slides down the wall, too.

"You're not different," she shrugs. "You're just special."

I roll my eyes. Leave it to Mom to try to spin this into something positive.

"Listen," she says after a minute of silence. "I know this isn't the gift you were hoping for, but it's the gift you got. You can't change that. You'll just need to learn how to use it in your favor. You know, figure out how to make it match your special."

I roll my eyes again, but this time, I lean into Mom a teensy bit. She takes the hint and uses her hand to gently push my head onto her shoulder.

"It took me years to really discover my magic," she says with a sigh. "I wish someone would've advised me to work on it earlier. I think a lot of things could be different today if I had."

I lift my head off her shoulder and turn to give her a confused look. What is she talking about?

She purses her lips together and pats my hand in between hers, then stands back up and starts to walk away.

"Mom?" I ask, making my eyes as big and sweet-looking as I possibly can.

Mom looks over her shoulder at me.

"Do you think I'll ever be able to go to the blomalfur village? You know, just to see if I feel less different there?"

Mom bites her bottom lip and her eyes fill with tears.

This isn't the first time I've asked to go to Plethora, so why is Mom acting so weird about it today?

"Sweetheart." Dad comes marching into the room from out of nowhere and wraps his arm around Mom's shoulder. "Did you just ask what I think you did?" His voice does not sound happy.

"It's okay," Mom tries to calm him down.

He shakes his head. "Tinsey," he scolds. "You know we can't talk about this. It's one thing to dream about stuff like that when you're ten, but you're eleven now. You just came into an amazing gift. It's time to accept that this is the way things are."

"But…" I begin.

Dad cuts me off right away. "Trealfurs don't mingle with blomalfurs," he says, adding an extra ounce of disgust to the word *blomalfurs*. "You know that. You've always known that, Tinsey. It's not going to change. Not now, not ever."

"But," I try again, determined to finish my thought this time. "Trealfurs don't mingle with *any* other huldufolk. I've never even met a blomalfur. Or a yuleman. Or a troll!" I stomp my foot. "It's not fair!"

"Sweetheart," Dad says, his voice a teensy bit gentler, but not much. "We've talked about this a hundred times before."

It's true, we have. One hundred and three to be exact.

"Things have been this way since I was a little boy," he explains. "All the different huldufolk in the Bungaborg used to interact freely with each other, but all that stopped when King Clover, your grandfather and ruler of the trealfurs way back then, declared he was closing the walls of Snugglepunk. He felt very strongly that our people were the superior race in the forest. He didn't see why the trealfurs should continue to put themselves at risk by interacting with the less friendly, more dangerous communities. So, he shut the rest of Bungaborg off from Snugglepunk."

"I know," I roll my eyes. After hearing a story a hundred and three times, it's hard not to. "Grandpa Clover created the Snugglepunk Safety Stone with his magic and placed it on the biggest tree to protect us all from dangerous outsiders."

At the mention of the gemstone, Dad mumbles the same mantra we all said in the circle earlier. It takes everything inside me not to laugh. I'm still not convinced there's anything up there in that largest tree.

"And," I continue, "he built up our vine walls to be taller than the rest of the faery ring. Blah, blah, blah. So, everyone got the point and left us alone. I get it. But, that king's been dead for a long time, so why are we still following his ideas?"

Dad shrugs. "Your mom's brother doesn't think much differently about the other huldufolk."

"King Vondur has our best interests at heart, sweetie," Mom chimes in, her voice still sounding forced. "After we closed our walls, stories started spreading about how aggressive the sprites and yulemen became. Everyone got really offended that we shut them out."

"And, you've heard the rumors that trolls have started to eat any trealfur that crosses their paths, right?" Dad asks with a shudder. "It's just not worth the risk of leaving."

"That's right," Mom agrees. "Besides, things have worked out okay this way. And, it's important to follow King Vondur's decisions."

"Yeah, but how does anyone really know if all these other huldufolk are really dangerous if nobody's seen them for tons of years? I mean, what if everyone out there thinks trealfurs are evil, too? Only, we're not. And they probably aren't, either."

Dad sighs. Likely because he's heard this argument from me one hundred and three times.

"Just trust that we're safer right here," he says. "That's enough for now."

"Yeah, only it's not!" I yell, surprising myself. I don't usually get so riled up during this conversation. I guess I'm feeling extra sensitive given the happenings of the day. "Things aren't all hunky dory or whatever because there are kids like me." I point to myself, which is silly because of course everyone knows who I'm referring to, but I can't help myself. "Kids who feel trapped in their towns. Kids who want to see what else is out there."

"That's enough," Mom warns me from her corner.

I don't take the hint, though. I'm on a total roll.

"Now that I'm so grown up," I spit, "I think I can make my own decisions, thank you very much."

"Enough!" Dad yells. Our entire cave shakes with his echo. I can practically see the smoke billowing out of his ears as his face turns a dark red. His eyeballs even fill with little pink veins. Yikes. Maybe I took things a bit too far. My heart races like it's trying to escape a dreki dragon. This is not going to end well if I stick around any longer. I sprint outside and away from my home, hoping my feet can run as quickly as my heart.

CHAPTER SIX

What I wouldn't give for Aspen's gift now. If only I could call a fox to come whisk me away from all this. I form my mouth into a little circle like I've seen my brother do and try to make some sort of pitch that sounds even remotely like the noises he creates to summon animals.

"Boopity, bop!" I squeak. Nope, that's not right. "Weeple, woople!" Nope, still sounds strange. "Blupper, burple?"

I shake my head with a huff. This isn't working. Once I'm calmed down a bit, I notice a rustle of leaves overhead. Wait! Did something actually understand me? I squint to see better. Another shake in the tree. A very slow shake. A sleek, gray tail sulks down from a branch and into view. Great. Of all the forest creatures I could have attracted, a tiny field mouse is the only thing to respond.

"Hey, Fred," I call up with a half-hearted wave.

Fred the mouse has been my friend forever. He's the only animal who understands me. I mean, we don't talk each other's language or anything like that, but we just *get* each other. Fred's one of my favorite things about Snugglepunk.

"Sorry, Fred," I cup my hands over my mouth and shout up into the tree. "But, I'm afraid I'm on the hunt for something a little bigger. No offense!"

Fred nods. He always understands. He disappears back up into the tree.

I guess I'm just going to have to use my own two feet. I run past a group of kids my age who are scrubbing the base of a tree with blades of grass. I try my best to sneak around them, but for the second time in one day, I'm found out. Maybe I'm not as expert a sneaker as I originally thought.

"Hey, Tinsey!" one of the kids hollers. "I heard about the council meeting today. Nice work on your gift. That's awesome!"

"Yeah," another chimes in. "Super cool power! It'll save you tons of time on your chores!"

I ignore them completely and run even faster. Well, I don't actually run any faster because I'm already going as quickly as I possibly can, but in my mind lightning bolts shoot out from my feet. Forty-four paces at thirty degrees, then a hundred and seven at ninety degrees. I hardly need to count as I go, and I don't slow down until I get to the opening in the vines at the edge of Snugglepunk. If no one's going to give me permission to go to Plethora, I'll just have to figure it out myself. I mean, I'm bound to be grounded when I get back home anyway. At least this way I'll have had an adventure first.

But, what if Dad's right? What if the other huldufolk really are just as close-minded as the trealfurs when it comes to interacting with each other? I can't imagine that's true, but I have to be prepared just in case. Maybe I can somehow make myself look like a blomalfur so I'll blend in over there. But how? Blomalfurs must be at least four and one quarter times as tall as trealfurs and probably dress like flowers. I guess I don't actually know any of this for sure, but I'm betting it's true.

I mean, why wouldn't they decorate themselves in perfectly crafted clothes?

I look around for materials, but everything in Snugglepunk is so green and boring. Certainly nothing appropriate for blomalfur clothing. Maybe I can use my magic power to create something bright and bold? I snap my fingers and an odd-shaped grayish sponge falls out of the sky. I don't suppose that will do me any good to make myself look better.

My knees suddenly get all wobbly and give out, dropping me to the ground next to the sponge with an *oomph*! I forgot about that whole weakness bit that comes with using my new power. If only I'd thought to ask Mom for some of her lavender oil before I ran out of the house. Not like that would have been any more awkward than the way I actually did end that argument.

I sit up and press my hand to my throbbing forehead, wiping strands of purple locks out of the way. There's got to be a way to control my magic. That's what Mom said at least, right? It would be pretty cool if I could choose *which* cleaning product appeared when I snapped. I guess if I'm going to have this power, I may as well try to figure out how to use it in my favor.

I close my eyes and picture a cleaning rag, like the ones we weave together from the golden wheat stalks. It wouldn't be the most comfortable thing, but it'd work nicely as a blomalfur dress, I think. *Snap.* A giant broom falls out of the sky and lands with a thunk. So much for that. I squeeze my eyes shut even tighter and picture the head of a mop, all soft and cottony and made from a balled up spider web. Snap. Another giant broom drops down on the other side of me. This is *so* not going well.

I feel really dizzy now. I lay back and watch the leaves above me dance in the light breeze. When it gets windy enough, some of those leaves will even snap off their branch and get to fly away. Not me, though. I'm never going to get out of Snugglepunk.

I turn to face the broom on my right. I squint one eye and use my other to guesstimate the sweeper's size. It's got to be eight times my body, so probably just over four feet, give or take. I turn to face the broom on my left and give it the same quick guesstimate. Four feet. Well, my magic may be ridiculous, but at least it pops out consistently-sized products.

And then, just like that, an idea seeps into my mind. I ignore my lingering headache and sit straight up. Sure, it's a crazy thought, but it just might work.

CHAPTER SEVEN

"Tins?" Aspen's feet hit the ground with a *thump* as he jumps off the back of an Icelandic sheep. He's walking toward me, but I'm not quite ready to reveal myself. I stay hidden behind a tree and add the final touch to my disguise. Maybe I'll even fool Aspen into thinking I'm actually a blomalfur!

"Ta da!" I waddle out from my hiding place.

"Waddling" is probably not the right word. "Stumbling" is more appropriate. I'm on top of the two long brooms I brought into existence with my new power and am walking on them like stilts. I've never been on stilts before, but I can say with one hundred percent certainty now, they're not easy to use.

"What in the world?" Aspen takes a step backward and gives me a look that says he thinks I've gone insane.

"Whaddya think?" I shout down.

"What are you doing on those things?"

"They're my new legs!" I cheer. "You know, to make me the same size as a blomalfur. Do you like 'em? The hardest part was figuring out how to strap vines to the broom bristles to wrap around my feet. In the end, it all came down to a simple calculation of weight distribution, but all in all, I'd say they look pretty realistic, don't you think?"

"You can't be serious..." Aspen slaps his hand onto his forehead. Once again, his blue hair doesn't move an inch away from perfection.

"Sorry," I yell. "I can't hear you from all the way up here." Even though I can.

"Tins," he says louder than before. "This is ridiculous. Sure, you're taller, but you still look nothing like a blomalfur. You just look like, well, a trealfur on top of giant brooms."

Brothers. Doesn't he even notice my awesome outfit?

"Check out my dress!" I call down again, sure that this time he'll realize how much I actually do look like a real blomalfur.

I spent the last hour smashing and smearing crabapples onto the least dead leaves I could find. I even tempted fate by sneaking up on a thistle bush and plucking a handful of the purple burrs. Those stuck nicely to the leaves.

"Yeah," Aspen snorts. "Of course I noticed your dress. It looks like you smeared poop all over a leaf."

Poop?! I look down at my outfit. Okay fine, so the berries didn't create the brightest costume in the world, but it definitely doesn't look like it's covered in poop...does it? I lift one foot up and then the other and stumble my way to a tree trunk, dragging the broom sticks along with me. Leaning against the tree, I'm able to unlace my stilts and climb back down to the ground.

"Do you think the blomalfurs would like me?" I ask, even though I already know what my brother's answer will be.

"Of course not," he says simply. Honestly.

"Why not?" I push my hands onto my hips, daring my brother to challenge me.

"Because, look at you," Aspen says. "I mean, I've

never seen a blomalfur or anything, but I can't imagine they look anything like this." He gestures toward me with his hands.

"Well," I counter, "who cares what I look like anyway. All that matters is that I think like a blomalfur. At least, I bet I do."

I drop my hands from my hips and feel my bottom lip tremble. Maybe I could come up with a different disguise? Aspen sighs, then takes a step closer to me. His face looks strange. Almost like he feels bad for shooting down my dreams.

"Sorry I said those things, kid," he says. "Listen, I didn't come here to fight with you."

I can't lie; I love when he calls me kid.

In a voice that tells me he's being totally serious, he whispers in my ear, "You're awesome just how you are, Tins. You know that, right?"

I feel the same warm, fuzzy feeling I get after solving an especially challenging equation. I nod, because I *do* know I'm awesome even though I'm different. I'm just not so sure the rest of the village agrees.

"You'll figure all this out, I'm sure of it," Aspen

says, as though he's answering a question nobody even asked.

"So, wait…" I say. "Are you saying I should keep working on a disguise to look like the blomalfurs? Does that mean you think I should leave Snugglepunk, too?"

Siblings can be complicated like that.

"That's not at all what I'm saying," Aspen scrunches his nose up. "I would never encourage you to go out there. It's dangerous, Tins."

I bite my bottom lip. So much for thinking he had my back.

"But listen," he says. "I do think you're totally right."

He does?

"I think the trealfurs could definitely use some updating in the way we're so closed off to everything around us. You're onto something really important, Tins."

I am?

"So," he says with a nod. "Keep being you, okay? People will start to listen. They'll have to. And hey, I bet you'll even change the world someday."

My lip quivers at his words. I sit up and lurch forward, grabbing my brother in a giant hug and getting crabapple smear all over him.

CHAPTER EIGHT

Aspen calls the sheep over and hops on its back.

"Stay here and hang out with me," I plead. This is really nice.

"Nah," he shakes his head. "Someone needs to go keep your adoring fans distracted when they all ask where the girl with the amazing new power got off to." He winks. "Just promise to be back home before nightfall so I don't have to worry about you, okay?"

I cross my heart with my finger. "Promise."

Aspen nods, then kicks the sheep's side and the two of them race out of sight.

Once he's gone, I play his pep talk over and over in my mind. He believes I can do anything. He really does, he said so himself. I can practically feel the confidence and courage coursing through my veins. I close my eyes and imagine myself having all the power in the entire world. If I can do anything, then I can safely make it to Plethora. My gut reminds me that's not what Aspen was suggesting, but I tell my gut to quiet down. I've got a plan to hatch. Maybe I don't need a disguise after all. In fact, I bet the blomalfurs will be so thrilled to see an actual, living trealfur, they'll welcome me in with open arms. Maybe even throw me a feast. My mouth waters.

Stay focused, I scold myself.

I promised I'd be home by nightfall, which gives me practically the entire day to go exploring. I wonder what the quickest way to get to Plethora is? I should probably go all the way around the faery ring to stay under the tree coverage. It would definitely be the safest option. But, it would take forever. I have no idea how big Bungaborg is, but I'm absolutely certain I couldn't walk around the perimeter of the Icelandic forest in a whole week, let alone a single day. I think about my perfect view of the blomalfur town from that opening in the vines. It's directly across the engi from here. I bet it would only take a couple hours at most to get there that way.

Since I silenced my gut, a tiny voice in the very back of my head pipes up and warns me about the engi. Everyone knows how dangerous it can be out there in the wide open. Especially for someone my size. But, before that little voice has a chance to state its case more loudly, my legs jump into action. Literally. In no time flat, I'm running at top speed toward that opening in the overgrown vines. I'm pretty certain I'll stop when I get there, but my feet have a different idea. They keep padding quickly forward. The opening in the vines gets bigger as I get closer. Bigger. Bigger. And then, just like that, I'm outside of Snugglepunk. I'm actually on the other side! I can't see a single thing, though. In fact, I can't even keep my eyes open for more than a second at a time in the direct sunlight. Red dots dance around the insides of my eyelids and my cheeks instantly burn up to at least a hundred and five degrees. So this is what those greedy trees have been keeping from me. Beautiful, glorious, scalding hot sunshine.

Covering my face with one hand, I reach back with the other and tug at a leaf on one of the vines behind me until it breaks off with a snap. I wrap it around my head like a hood and my cheeks feel cooler immediately. My eyes also relax and open wider. I can see everything now.

There aren't trees or leaves anywhere. Only tall, wispy grasses, different shades of green and yellow weeds, and flowers of all different sizes and colors, which is all cool but terribly underwhelming compared to the rich blue sky. I've never seen anything like it before. It's so beautiful I could cry. But, I don't because I have some serious work to do. I know exactly which direction to go to get to Plethora. At least I thought I did. Out here in the wide open, I'm suddenly not so certain. I squint and look around at the continuous faery ring along the horizon. I look for the shimmering trees of Plethora, but all the faraway trees seem full of glitter from this angle. If only there was someone here to ask for directions, but I'm the only living creature around. Well, except for a gray puffball of a rabbit with one black ear hopping around like a fool. That thing wouldn't be of any help, I'm sure. It looks lost itself. I try to drum up my geography lessons. Snugglepunk is the most northern village in Bungaborg. West of us is Bobbyknock, the yulemen town. Rumplelawn, where the trolls live, is on the east end, and Plethora is south of Snugglepunk. Directly below Dreki Mountain.

I find the peak of the snowy volcano above the horizon—the smoke puffing out of the top is visible in the bright blue sky. My eyes lower back down the skyline to a thick clump of trees. They're definitely shimmering in the sunlight. That's got to be Plethora!

I set off in the direction I now know I'm supposed to be moving and try my best to stay on course. It's really hard, though. Turns out, walking in a perfectly straight line through a seemingly endless field of nothing but weeds isn't so simple. Maybe I underestimated how long this would actually take. At least there's all sorts of cool new stuff to take in. The dusty smell of the dry grasses, the spreading heat of sunbeams on the back of my hand. The screeching cry of a gyrfalcon piercing through the sky directly overhead. Wait, what!

I shoot my face upward hoping it's not true, but no such luck. Right there dirtying up the clear blue sky with its circling movement is an enormous brown predatory bird.

CHAPTER NINE

REEEK! The falcon cries out.

My heart pounds its response. This is so not good! My head begs my feet to run, but my feet give a firm *no*. Maybe they're right. Maybe I should stay put. I rack my brain. What action are you supposed to take when you're the prey of a large bird? Lie down and play dead? Run like the dickens? I can't remember. Probably because I never learned that. There was no need under the canopy of the faery ring. Anyway, I guess it doesn't matter one way or another because the falcon's clearly seen me and is diving. My feet finally decide to run.

Of course, trealfur legs are nowhere near fast enough when it comes to giant flying predators. The bird scoops me right up into its rough claws, then lifts me high into the same sky I was just admiring. Who knew I'd see it for the first time and be carried away into it all in one day? Too bad I can't enjoy the view more. Or even at all. The falcon's talons cup over me and dig into my sides a little bit. I yip in pain, but my voice just bounces off the claw wall around me. Saying this situation is awful is the understatement of the century. If only Aspen were with me, he'd be able to explain everything to this animal and surely the bird would let me go.

"CAW! CAW!" I scream up, hoping that maybe, just maybe, I can suddenly speak with this creature. My voice bounces off its tightly clasped talons and right back into my face. Oh well. What would I even want the falcon to do at this point? Let me go? No way. I'd fall straight to my death. The only hope I have with my silly power would be to build a tower of cleaning supplies high enough to reach me. If a broom is roughly four feet tall, it would probably take twenty-four snaps to create enough of them to stack up tall enough to get to me. The bird would be in such shock, it'd have to let me go, then I'd saunter down the broom ladder all the way to safety. Of course, the chances of me being able to summon a broom when I actually want to are slim to none. Plus, a whole ladder of them that wouldn't topple right over? Fat chance.

Think. Think. Think. My best chance of survival at this point is to just hang tight and wait till we get back to its nest. From there, I can use my sneaking skills to dart away and down the tree. Yeah, that should work. Unless of course this bird has babies. In that case, I'm toast. Yeesh, I can't believe my day went from hoping I'd get to meet a real blomalfur to thinking about becoming a hatchling's dinner.

Suddenly, something shifts. Even though I can't see where we're going, the lurch of my stomach tells me we're dropping downward. Quickly. Too quickly. What's happening? The gyrfalcon lets out the same squawk it did when it was chasing me, although it sounds much more muffled from this talon cage. I can't help but wonder if it sees a juicier, fatter snack. Maybe it spotted that fluffy rabbit I saw earlier. For once in my life, I thank my lucky stars I'm so tiny. Maybe now I'll live to see my twelfth birthday! The bird loosens its hold on me and I start to slip. First my right leg, then my left. Followed by my rear end, then my belly. Finally, my entire body slides through the scratchy talons and straight into a free fall. I don't dare look down, but I really hope I'm not too far off the ground.

Sure enough, the falcon completely forgets about me once I'm flailing through the air. It leaves me helpless and dives past me to catch something more appealing. I brace myself for the crash landing, but to my surprise, when I finally do hit the ground, my brains don't splat out of my head. In fact, I don't crash onto a hard surface at all. Instead, I start sinking. Yes, sinking! I'm falling straight down into something thick, warm, and sticky. It's like I'm getting eaten up by quicksand. Really muddy quicksand.

CHAPTER TEN

I can't quite decide which is worse: getting carried away by a hungry bird, or sinking down into a pond of brown slime. Either way, I'm beginning to feel like today just isn't my day. My fox bowling for trealfurs at the council meeting, my strange gift presenting itself in front of everyone...wait... My strange gift! I can clean things up with the snap of my fingers! And, what needs cleaning up more than a giant puddle of mud?

I try to push my pointer finger and thumb together, but it's not happening. The mud has me in such a strong hold. I can't move a single muscle in my body. Well, except for my eyelids since my head's still above the surface. I can blink. And my nostrils can flair, too. I open and shut my mouth just to check those muscles. I try to wiggle my ears, but they don't move. That's not a cause for concern though; I've never been able to wiggle my ears. Okay, fine. So, I can work some of my muscles, just not the ones I need to move right now. My body slinks farther down into the mud, which makes my throat gulp on its own. One more muscle that still works. But, the truth is, if I can't create a snap, I won't be able to use any of my muscles soon enough because they'll all be underneath this sludge in no time flat.

Come on! I beg my fingers to find each other. All I need is one little snap.

My throat sinks below the surface and I lift my face up to keep it above, but the mud keeps rising up my neck. It seeps past my chin, followed by my mouth. I take in a huge breath of air through my nose before that sinks down into the slime, too. I close my eyes and feel them get covered as well, until finally even the top of my head is beneath the goop. I'm already losing my breath and know I won't be able to hold the air in much longer. For the second time today, I'm certain I won't make it to my twelfth birthday.

My lungs are about to explode. They beg me to just breathe out. Just breathe out. They have no idea the situation we're in. Otherwise I'm sure they wouldn't force me to do such things. Just. Breathe. Out.

I have no choice. I follow the order and let out a teensy exhale. Maybe if I release the air slowly enough, it will buy me some more time to think. A string of tiny bubbles blows through the mud with my breath and I feel the muck swirl around me and loosen the slightest bit. Wait. Air bubbles can push through this stuff? Could my breath be strong enough to help me? I know it's a long shot, but I don't have much of a choice. I blow out roughly eighty percent of the air stored up in my lungs. A giant bubble forms and shoots out of my mouth and up toward the surface. The mud shifts along its course, which gives my hand just enough wiggle room to touch my pointer finger and my thumb together. A silent snap.

Please, please, please work. I'm almost completely out of air now. My lungs beg me to inhale. *Stop being so selfish!* I scold them in my mind. And then, I notice a ripple in the mud. Something's pushing down on it from the surface! Did my feeble attempt at a snap work? And what in the world did it summon? Suddenly, the top of my head feels the sweet breeze again. My eyes are next. I open them when I'm certain they're not submerged by mud anymore and see an army of light brown sponges working hard to sop up this puddle of muck. As the sludge lowers inch by inch, my body continues to feel the bliss of freedom. Even though my whole body feels weak from using my power, my nose is still able to take in a huge breath of air. *Thank you, thank you, thank you!*

In no time at all, the now engorged sponges clean up the whole mud pit, leaving me completely out of energy in the middle of a large, dry hole.

Thanks, I think again, smiling toward the sponges, even though it seems a little ridiculous to show any sort of gratitude toward such a thing as that. They disappear in a puff of sparkles. Once the sparkles dissipate, I look around at my surroundings. Where am I? Huge willow trees with snot-green branches droop down like slime all around me. Peppered across the swampy ground as far as I can see are tons and tons of little mud pits just like the one I was stuck in. Everything's so ugly and straight up messy.

Uh oh. The reality hits me one second too late.

"Wut's dat?!" A voice just as nasty as the environment around me booms nearby.

I turn with wide eyes to see the most hideous creature I could ever imagine.

CHAPTER ELEVEN

I notice the troll's feet first. Curled green toenails attached to fat, beige toes that are shaped more like bricks. I can't tell for sure sitting in this dried-up pit, but I'm guessing I come up to this monster's calves at best. A twelfth his size, maybe. My eyes keep drifting upward as I beg my legs to regain their energy ASAP. The same beige skin hangs loosely off this guy's entire body, like he's made of undercooked oatmeal cookie. His dark eyes aren't positioned evenly on his face and his nose is just as wonky. Don't even get me started on his mouth: No lips, just a ragged hole filled with yellow corn-on-the-cob teeth. Gross, right?

"Iz you's a trealfur?" the troll asks, smacking his black, slug-like tongue over his lips, or at least over the area where his lips should be. His voice is just as disgusting as the rest of him.

I think quickly. "I most certainly am not." The lie rolls out in my most confident voice.

Maybe he doesn't know what a trealfur actually looks like. If he thinks I'm something different, perhaps he won't chomp me up whole.

"I am…um…a yuleman. Yes, that's right. I'm a yuleman." I puff out my chest and throw my hands to my hips.

Please don't know the difference. Please don't know the difference.

"Ohhh…" the troll looks genuinely convinced. "Sorry fer da mistake," he shrugs. "I ain't never seena trealfur."

I nod. I totally understand. Up until five seconds ago, I'd never seen a troll before, either. But, at least I'm smart enough to know one when I see one.

"Wellll," he squints his droopy eyes, "no madder wut you's iz, wut er ya doin' in Rumplelawn?"

It's a fair question. I could spend an hour explaining everything, but I decide to go for the short version instead.

"I was attacked by a falcon that dropped me here," I say. Just saying it out loud makes my knees go weak all over again.

"Dat's awful!" The troll gasps. A string of slime stretches from his top teeth to his bottom. *Gross.*

Even still, it feels oddly comforting having someone to talk to about my traumatic day.

"It *was* awful," I confirm. "You can't even imagine!"

"Wellll, why doncha come home wiff me's? I cans at least give you's a good meal."

My tummy rumbles at his mention of food.

"Bedder dan sittin' round here in dis ugly hole. I swears dis thing use ta be a bootiful mud puddle."

I nod sheepishly. There's no way I'm telling this guy I summoned sponges out of nowhere to get rid of all that nasty mud he seems to love so much. He reaches his enormous hand out to me, palm up, inviting me to climb aboard. Maybe it's crazy, but I can't think of a single reason not to go with him. I mean, what do I have to lose? I've already faced death twice today. What are the odds it would happen a third time? Plus, he seems convinced I'm a yuleman. I hope trolls don't like eating yulemen, although I guess no one's ever told me that. I look at his bumpy hand. It would definitely be nice to get a free ride through Rumplelawn with someone who knows his way around. Kind of like my own personal tour guide. It would certainly keep me from nearly drowning in another mud pit, especially since my legs still feel pretty weak. My stomach growls again and that makes up my mind. I pull myself up and into his palm.

"Soo," he says as he strides through the disgusting town of Rumplelawn. "Are's yulemen really as cheeky's as everyone says?"

"I dunno, I've never met one," I shrug.

He tilts his head and gives me a confused look. "But," he says. "You's iz a yuleman, right?

Right.

"Uh," I try to recover. "What I mean to say is, I've never met a yuleman *who isn't cheeky.* Of course."

He smiles. Whew. That was a close one.

"How about trolls?" I ask. "Are they really as messy as everyone says?"

"Whaddya you's think?" He laughs and uses his free hand to motion to the scenery. "Izn't it bootiful?"

I look around. Slime, worms, and mud everywhere.

"Yeah," I say. "It's really something…"

I can't think of anything else to say about the matter, so I change the subject.

"Do trolls really think trealfurs taste like candy?" I ask, but immediately regret my choice to change the subject to that.

"Wut??" He looks offended. "Dat's just silly. I ain't never eated a single trealfur in me whole life. In facts, I've never even mets one! None of us trolls has. I ain't never heards such a ridiculous lie. Trolls is bugatarians of course. We don'ts eat nothin' but vegetables an' bugs."

Really? I squint up at him to see if he's fibbing. Why would everyone tell me trolls love eating trealfurs if it isn't true? The brute looks serious, though. Sincere even.

"What do yulemen eat?" He asks, catching my eye. "Wait jus' a minute, do you's likes ta eats trealfurs? is dat why's yer askin'?" His eyes grow wide with intrigue.

"Pssh, of course not!" I scoff. "We eat...uh... you know, berries and stuff."

I actually have no idea what yulemen eat, but I think someone once told me they like berries. Then again, someone once told me trolls love eating trealfurs, so I'm starting to feel a bit uncertain about some of the things I've heard.

"What's your name?" I ask, determined once again to chance the subject.

"Oh me's goodness," he throws his free hand against his forehead. "Where's me manners. Me name's Judder. Judder Slimer. Whadda bout you's?"

"Nice to meet you Judder." I grab onto his brick-like pinkie finger and give it a tug, like I'm shaking his hand. "I'm Tinsey Clover."

CHAPTER TWELVE

Judder's cave matches everything else I've seen in Rumplelawn. Take, for example, his kitchen table. There are rotting tree trunks positioned as chairs around a giant rock covered in hairy moss the color and texture of shriveled-up worms that dried in the sun. See what I mean? Rumplelawn is downright disgusting.

"'ello?" Judder calls out as we enter the space.

No answer.

"Good," he mumbles. "Don' wan's no one ta gets in me's way."

He slides me down on top of the wormy table then swipes his arm up toward the cave ceiling through a thick clump of spider webs. A few of the glistening threads wrap around his hand.

"Here's ya go," he says, balling up the dusty silk and plopping it down next to me. "A 'iddle cushion fer yer's bottom while's I cooks." He licks his lips, which makes me shudder.

What if he actually knows I'm a trealfur and was lying to me about not wanting to eat me? Did I just get outsmarted by a troll? I force a smile and clamor onto the spiderweb bean bag he made me. Something in my gut warns me not to freak out while Judder's watching me. Once he turns his back, I can come up with a getaway plan.

The troll shuffles away, toward a stone fire pit on the other end of the cave. He rubs some sticks together and produces a flame in the pit, then pulls out all sorts of vegetables from a small wooden crate. The smell of coriander fills the cave and my stomach goes totally crazy with hunger. *Don't get too excited*, I warn my belly. *We could be the main course!* I try to focus on coming up with a way to escape, but it's nearly impossible as I watch Judder slice and chop carrots and celery with unbelievable precision. His motions are mesmerizing. Who knew such brutish hands could work so artistically? He even peels a radish around and around until it looks exactly like a tiny rose!

"I'm almos' dun, 'iddle friend!" he sings out, looking beyond content in his own little cooking world over there.

I continue to watch in awed silence. Judder turns his attention to a gigantic pot of stew or something like that. Whatever it is, it must be thick because it takes both of his hands wrapped around his giant wooden spoon to stir. The extra work doesn't seem to bother him at all, though. In fact, it looks like he's loving every minute of it. He's so distracted now, it would be a great time to escape. But, I can't bring myself to move. It's too much fun watching this troll do what he clearly loves. This cheesy grin spreads across his face and then, get this, he starts in on a song. Yes, for real.

Gots ta get da veggies chopped,
Gots ta eat dem bugssss!
Gots ta stir da soup in pots,
Before we turn ta slugssss!

I have to say, I really hope his cooking is better than his singing. I've never fully appreciated the musical skills all the trealfurs have until this very minute. Well, all the trealfurs but me. I guess I'm not one to judge anyone else's singing abilities.

"Nice tune!" I call out, more sarcastically than I intend.

"Ya like it?" Judder beams, clearly not noticing my tone. "I's made it up all by me self!"

I couldn't tell.

"Wanna hear da next verse?"

I shake my head no, but it turns out he doesn't actually care whether or not I want to hear more of his song. He rolls right into the next verse:

When's da bugs is nice an' crisp,
I eatss dem with a spoooon!
Cookin' gives me's so much bliss,
Dat's why me's sings dis toooon!

I can't help but say it. That was seriously the worst thing I've ever heard.

"Finishin' touches!" Judder calls just as my ears stop ringing from his song.

He sprinkles something or other on top of the

platter of veggies then ladles his stew into two bowls made from the shells of gourds and brings them over to the table, still humming his melody.

"Eats up!" he urges, pushing a bowl into my stomach.

Smelling the stew up close makes it easy to forgive this troll's tone deaf singing. One whiff and it's like my nose fell asleep and is having the best dream of its life. I don't even wait for a spoon before plunging my entire face straight into the bowl. Mom would not be proud of my table manners. She'd for sure say the slurping and smacking sounds coming out of my mouth are downright embarrassing. I don't care one bit, though. I'd make twenty times the grunts if that's what it took to get another bite of this heavenly stew.

"Whoa, slow down der, 'iddle friend!" Judder laughs. "Der's plenty fer us all, I's promise."

I try to obey his words, but I can't stop. "This is incredible!" I gasp in the two second break I take from devouring the food.

He blushes through his rough skin.

"Awww, stop it," he says shyly.

"No, I'm serious. This is the best food I've ever eaten, like, in my entire life! I wouldn't lie about something like that." I really wouldn't.

I almost ask him what's in it, but I decide against it. After hearing his song about cooking with bugs, I have a feeling I'd rather not know all the ingredients.

"You have a real talent," I keep the compliments coming. "Do you cook for other people?"

Judder's face falls. Uh oh. Did I say something wrong?

"What?" I ask, forcing myself away from the stew, which is no easy task.

"Nuttin'" he shrugs, even though it's clear it's not *nuttin'*. "It's jus' dat...well, alls I've ever wanted ta do's iz ta becomes a chef, but dat's not wut trolls is supposed ta be, ya knows? I'm supposed ta wanna throw mud all over everythin' an' stuff. Mom an' Dad won' even lemmee cook at all. Says it's only encouragin' me's silly thoughts an' takin' away from wut's importan'."

I use the back of my hand to wipe the soup off

my lip. And my cheek. And my eyebrows. I nod because I really truly know how Judder feels. Even though I'm smaller than most huldufolk, in that moment the whole Bungaborg Forest doesn't feel so big anymore. We sit in silence together for a minute, Judder with his oatmeal cookie face and me with my messy purple hair, and suddenly we don't seem so different from each other.

CHAPTER THIRTEEN

The sun's starting to dip down a little too low in the sky for comfort. For as scary as the engi is during the day, I can't even imagine how creepy it is at night. I've got to get home. I promised Aspen!

"Why doncha takes da faery ring route insteads?" Judder asks, scratching his head. "It's much safer."

I know he's right. "I don't have time for that!" I snap unintentionally.

"Okay," Judder raises his hands in surrender. "Yer choice, 'iddle friend. C'mon, I can's takes ya so's you gets there quickers."

I'm not about to refuse that offer. I hop back onto his hand and we stride through Rumplelawn. Judder stops by the slimy vines that wall out the engi.

"Sorry 'iddle friend," he says. "I jus' needs a minute ta wraps me head 'round goin' inta da engi at dusk. Id's jus' not a smart thing ta do."

He pats me on the top of my head. I can tell he's trying to be gentle, but his giant hand still pushes my neck down uncomfortably with every tap.

"Nice meetin' ya 'iddle friend," he says in a wobbly voice.

Why is he saying this now?

"Judder?" I ask. "Are you worried something bad will happen in the engi?"

"Nah," he shrugs. "Id's jus' gonna be easier ta say goodbye now's."

Fair enough.

"Nice to meet you, too," I give a little curtsey in his hand.

It chokes him right up.

"Listen, maybe I'll see ya 'round." I say, even though I know there's a very low probability of that. If I ever sneak out of Snugglepunk again, I certainly will not be visiting Rumplelawn. "And hey," I add. "You really should think about becoming a chef."

He opens his mouth to cut me off, but I put up my hand to silence him and continue.

"I know the other trolls aren't so psyched about it, but I'm starting to think that sometimes the people around us don't always know what's best for us. I mean, look at me. If I didn't sneak out of Snugglepunk today, I would've never met you!"

"Snugglepunk?" Judder raises an eyebrow. Or at least he would have if he had an eyebrow to raise. A sideways grin creeps across his mouth. "I knews you's was a trealfur and not's a yuleman. I did! Right from da very beginnin'."

I pinch my lips together. Oops. "Well, secret's out I guess," I shrug. "So…are you gonna eat me now?"

Judder rolls his eyes. "I already told's ya! Trolls don' eat trealfurs! But, wut are ya doin' outsides of yer's town? Everyone's knows trealfurs don' want nuttin' ta do wiff anyone else."

I bite my lower lip. I have to say, even though I know that's the truth, it hurts to hear someone outside of Snugglepunk say it aloud.

"Not all of us," I say softly.

Judder tilts his head like he's trying to understand. I force a smile, then use my chin to motion toward the engi. We should really get going. Judder starts walking again, and I can't help myself from humming his awful song as we go. What can I say, it's catchy.

Even in the fading daylight, I can see Snugglepunk off in the distance thanks to my grandpa's extra tall vine wall. It definitely looks unwelcoming, to say the least. Well, everything except for the large, blue glistening circle hanging from the biggest tree. Wait a minute. Is that the Snugglepunk Safety Stone? I can't believe it, it actually does exist! And it's beautiful. At least from the view way over here. I can't believe my grandpa used his magic to create an actual forcefield to keep the other huldufolk out of Snugglepunk. Everyone in the forest must think we're the evil ones. I turn back around to face Judder.

"We're not bad people," I say, completely out of nowhere.

Judder looks at me with confusion plastered on his face. "Okay," he says with a shrug.

"I mean," I stammer, looking down at his palm. "I know it may look like we're totally standoffish or whatever, but, well, it's just that my uncle…" I trail off when I look up and see Judder's face.

He's no longer paying any attention to me. His eyes are fixated on something in the sky.

"Whoa," he whispers.

I look upward as well. A shadow seemingly the size of the entire engi falls over us. A massive something fills the sky. Whoa is right.

"A falcon?" I ask. When Judder doesn't say anything, I answer my own question. "No way, far too big."

With the last little bits of dusk, I can't make out many details, but I definitely see the dark outline of wings. Enormous, pointy wings with what seem to be claws on the ends.

"It'z da Bungaborg Dreki," Judder says, a definite tremor in his voice.

A chill shoots up my spine. The Bungaborg Dreki? But doesn't that dragon live up on the side of the Dreki Volcano? What's it doing down here?

"Have you ever seen it before?" I whisper.

Judder shakes his head back and forth. "Nevers," he whispers back.

We both watch in a strangely awed silence. Even without being able to see it clearly, it's easy to see the dragon's graceful movements. I mean, sure, it's absolutely terrifying, but there's something oddly peaceful about the way it's cutting through the purple sky. Like a leaf that's been gently snapped off a branch with the wind and flies off to freedom. Poetic, right?

In an instant, everything changes, though. No more peaceful soaring. The dreki's neck lurches backward and starts jerking side to side, looking more like a worm in pain than a content leaf. What's happening? A thunderous sneeze snaps through the air and a spray of flames shoots out of its mouth and straight toward the tall walls of Snugglepunk.

No, no, NO! I watch the corner of my town light up in orange and red sparks, the flames dancing dangerously close to the Snugglepunk Safety Stone. So this is who's been starting the fires lately. But, what in the world does the Bungaborg Dreki have against the trealfurs? It's not like we've ever even interacted, how could we have gotten on each other's bad sides?

I have to tell someone, but my feet won't budge. They're just as shocked as the rest of me. And so, I just stare helplessly as the flames grow bigger. The dragon watches the flames rise for a second or two, then darts toward the biggest tree and snatches up the Snugglepunk Safety Stone in its huge talons. It does a halfway front flip in the air until it's facing the opposite direction, then shoots off into the falling night sky.

CHAPTER FOURTEEN

I scramble down from Judder's hand and start to run into the engi toward Snugglepunk. My home. Judder follows, easily catching up, then throws his hands around me and tackles me to the ground.

"Let me go!" I scream, kicking and biting like a rabid rodent.

He doesn't let me go. "You's can't just runs into da engi like dat," he scolds.

"What do you care?" I spit, still trying to break free of his grip. "You didn't seem to think it was a problem like two minutes ago."

"Wellll, dat wuz before there wuz a dreki flyin' 'round."

"I need to get home!" I scream. "I need to tell someone!"

"Doncha think they's already knows?" Judder

points with his undercooked chin toward Snugglepunk.

I look. The flames are significantly smaller than they were seconds ago. The trealfur fire crew must already be on it. I let myself breathe.

"I's can't let cha goes home tonight's," Judder says, loosening his grip around me, which allows me to breath even deeper. "It's jus' not safe."

"So, what do you suggest I do, then?"

"You's can come home's with me's." Judder says with a single nod.

I think of Aspen. I promised him I'd be home by nightfall. I think of my parents. They'll be worried sick. But, Judder's right. The sun's fully set now and the sky's turning less purple and more black. Trying to go home at this point would be a really bad idea. I climb into Judder's outstretched hands and he carries me back to his slimy cave.

"Jus' be quiet, okay?" he whispers as we approach his front entrance. "Me's parents won't be so happy dat I's brought a 'iddle friend back. 'Specially not a trealfur."

I feel the same hurt I felt earlier at his negative

mention of trealfurs, but I nod and purse my lips shut nice and tight anyway. Judder cups his hands completely closed around me and we walk into his home.

Mumble, mumble, mumble. I hear a low-pitched voice saying something, but can't make out what through Judder's closed fingers. *Mumble, mumble.* I recognize Judder's voice answer back. *Mumble, mumble, mumble.* An even lower voice chimes in before Judder starts moving again.

"Me's parents are goin' ta bed nows. Hang in there, 'iddle friend." Judder opens his hands up just enough to relay that message to me, then he snaps them back shut again.

As I sit there in the dark, I try not to notice how Judder's palms are starting to get clammy, and not just a little bit. In fact, sweat is full on dripping down right on my head. Disgusting. *Think of something else*, I tell myself. *Anything else.* It doesn't take much. My mind quickly wanders back to the visual of that dreki ripping my grandpa's gemstone out of the tree. My mom will be devastated. The whole village will be. That stone represents my people's legacy. My family's legacy. That dragon will pay for this, no question.

After what feels like forever, Judder finally opens his hands and sets me free. I'm drenched from head to toe in stinky troll sweat. There's no way I'm sleeping like this.

"Mind if I do something real quick?" I ask Judder tentatively.

He shrugs.

I snap my fingers as quietly as I can. Both Judder and I watch as an enormous wet wheat-stalk rag forms above our heads in a poof of sparkles. Where was that when I was trying to make blomalfur clothes? The rag falls right toward me, landing on top of my entire body and trapping me in yet another wet enclosure. At least this one smells like fresh lemons. I was more hoping to summon a bit of soap or something, but I guess this'll work. After all, it's efficient. Judder gasps and lifts the cloth off me. It evaporates in his pinched fingers.

"Wut wuz dat?" He asks.

"Just my goofy magical power," I shrug.

He looks at me with a blank stare.

"You know," I continue. "The gift we all get around our eleventh birthdays?"

Still the blank stare. Do trolls not gain magical powers? Do any of the other huldufolk gain magical powers? I guess I've never thought about that before. Maybe being born a trealfur is cooler than I give it credit for.

I open my mouth to ask about it, but my body goes all weak. My knees buckle and I fall to the ground. I really don't like this whole magic power thing. It's so not worth feeling this yucky afterward. If only I could curl up in my own bed. I mean, it's not like my bed's anything more than a pile of leaves, but still. It's *my* pile of leaves. I wish Mom could wrap me up in her arms and give me some of that lavender oil to strengthen me. Maybe she would even sing me a lullaby and rock me to sleep.

"Are you's okay, 'iddle friend?" Judder asks.

I wipe my nose and pat my cheeks. I didn't realize I was crying.

"I'm fine," I sniff. "It's just, well, I've never slept away from home before."

Judder nods like he understands.

"Every night before bed, my family sings a little song together," I say. "I know it's silly or whatever, but every trealfur does the same thing at the same time and it makes us all feel connected." I look out the cave entrance at the pitch-black night. "Tonight's the first night of my life I haven't done that."

Judder sucks up a sob of his own. "Dat's really sad fer ya's," he says. "I's heard dat song before, id's bootiful. You's trealfurs sure does have pretty voices."

"Wait, what?"

"You's all have pretty voices," he says again.

"No, not that," I say. "I mean, you've heard us singing before? But, how?"

Judder looks at me like I'm missing out on something really obvious.

"Da whole forest can's hears yer song every night. It carries on da wind, ya knows. Helps puts us alls ta sleep."

As if on cue, a very faint chanting starts outside. I stand up and walk to the entrance of the cave.

Sure enough, I hear the tune we sing every single night before bed. It does sound lovely from all the way over here. I hum along even though my notes aren't anywhere close to on-pitch. Judder stands up and walks to my side. He starts humming along, too, possibly even more out of tune than me.

CHAPTER FIFTEEN

"Up en atum, 'iddle friend!"

The sound of a wooden spoon clangs on the cave wall. I open one eye, then the other. The glorious smell of sautéing greens and garlic fills the air. Where am I?

"I made you's breakfast!" Judder cheers.

I lift my head up and look around. The sun's shooting rays through the doorway of the troll cave. Right. I slept in Rumplelawn last night.

"If you's eats quick, you's can gets through da engi an' back home 'fore da sun gets too hot."

I smile at Judder. Who knew trolls could be so thoughtful? I should be getting home, but the light of the day gives me a new sense of courage.

"I'm not going back to Snugglepunk right away," I say casually.

Judder drops the spoon in surprise. "Wut? Why nots?" he asks.

"Because," I say. "I have something else to do first."

My troll friend takes a seat on the floor next to me.

"That dreki took my village's most sacred artifact. I can't just sit back and let that happen."

"But, why don' cha go homes and tells yer leaders wut you's saw? Dey's probably's knows whats ta do better dan you's."

I'd thought of that. "No one knows I left Snugglepunk yesterday," I say. "If I told anyone what I saw last night, I'd be grounded for life, no question. I can't very well help get the gemstone back if that happens, right?

Judder doesn't look convinced.

"I mean, that's only part of it, I guess," I admit. "I'm also worried that if Uncle Vondur finds out it was the Bungaborg Dreki who started all the fires, I think he might try to kill it. He's not the nicest of guys."

"Id's a dreki," Judder says. "Dat did somethin' bad."

"Yeah, I know, but I just don't want to be the one responsible for it getting hurt."

Judder twists his mouth up, like he almost understands, but not quite.

"I just need to try to get that stone back first." I say. "And, who knows? Maybe that dreki isn't so bad after all. Maybe it didn't actually mean to start that fire."

I can't believe I just suggested that.

"Who's knows," Judder shrugs. "I means, looks at us. I was sure's all trealfurs were unapproachable's or whatevers."

"Yeah, and I would have never believed a troll could cook."

"An' I thought's all trealfurs could sing," Judder teases with a laugh.

Low blow.

"It's only a matter of time before Uncle Vondur figures out it's the dreki lighting the fires. Who knows what he'll do to it." I cringe just thinking about it. "I've got to get to the dragon first."

I stand up and walk to the sautéed greens and shove a handful in my mouth.

"So, I don't know about you, but I'm going to Dreki Mountain," I declare.

"But," Judder says. "Wut if da dragon fries you's to a crisp?"

Of course that's a very real possibility. I can't think about that, though. I shove another fistful of greens into my mouth. The garlic adds an extra pop that covers all my tastebuds in just the right way. Perfection.

"So, how's you gonna gets ta Dreki Mountain, huh? It'd takes ya days ta walk there on yer 'iddle legs. Maybe's even weeks!"

He has a point. And then, an idea hits me.

"You're right," I reply. "I'm far too small to do something like this on my own."

He nods in agreement.

"What I'm really gonna need is a great sidekick."

He nods again.

"Someone who's big and strong and really, really smart. Someone who's been free to roam the forest his whole life and knows his way around way better than I ever could. Oh, and someone with dashing good looks wouldn't hurt." Okay fine, so I exaggerate a little bit.

Judder's nods slow down as my words sink in.

"Plus," I continue, "it wouldn't hurt if my sidekick was really great at cooking. That way, we won't starve on our journey."

Judder pushes his mouth to one side of his face.

"Nooo ways," he says, putting his hands on his hips. "Nooo ways, nooo hows."

I shrug, toss another pinch of greens into my mouth, and wipe my hands on my leaf shirt.

"Okay, then. Guess I'll just have to go it alone." I turn to leave. "Wish I could say 'see ya again,' but we both know that's pretty unlikely since I'll probably be dreki food by the end of the day."

"Wait," Judder says, taking my bait. "I can'ts lets ya do dat. I'd feel horribles." He pauses for a second and stares at the blank wall in front of him. "Okay's, fine." He nods. "I'lls come with you's."

I clap my hands together and can't hide the smile on my face. Before thinking it through, I run over to the troll and give his calf a big hug.

CHAPTER SIXTEEN

I march out of the cave and straight ahead, back toward the engi. Judder stops me with a pinch of his fingers against my shirt.

"Nooo way," he says. "No engi today."

"But, it'll be the quickest," I insist.

"An' da mos' dangerous. You's said it yerself, I know da forest better dan you's. If you's wants me's ta comes with you's, you's gonna have ta let me lead."

Fair enough.

"Fine," I say with a wave of my hand. "Lead away."

We walk through the thick of the droopy trees. I don't make it very far on my own before Judder picks me up and places me on top of his shoulder.

The slimy willow trees slowly become sparser as

we stride out of Rumplelawn. Lush, large birches take their place above and bright green heather moss replaces the soggy mud of the troll village. It's similar to Snugglepunk, which means I can't see the sky at all. Or Dreki Mountain.

"Are you sure we're going the right way?" I ask. I still don't understand why we couldn't have gone through the engi. Dreki Mountain's perfectly clear from there.

"A course I'm a' sure," Judder mumbles. "We's headin' to da south a' Bungaborg. I been dis way a millions a' times."

The south of Bungaborg. Why does that sound so familiar? It doesn't make any sense. With Snugglepunk in the north end of the faery ring, why would I feel anything toward the south? The scenery answers my question before my mind can. Perfectly spaced aspen trees, shimmering like glitter in the morning sunlight, just like they do from my little peephole in the vines. Only much, much closer this time. Plethora! With all the dragon stuff going on, I'd almost forgotten all about this place! Almost.

"Can we stop here for a minute?" I tap on Judder's shoulder.

"I thought we's needed ta get ta Dreki Mountain ta gets yer stone as quickly as possible," Judder says. "Why'd ya wanna waste any time's here?"

Because I'm in love with blomalfur elves, I think. *Because I'm one hundred percent certain I was supposed to be born a blomalfur instead of a trealfur.*

I don't say either of these things aloud.

"I dunno," I shrug, trying to act like it's not a big deal even though my heart's screaming inside. "I guess I've just always wanted to see what Plethora's like, that's all."

Judder stops cold. Uh oh. Did I say something wrong?

"Why's Plethora?" He asks.

I keep my mouth shut.

"Did's ya ever wanna see's Rumplelawn befores?"

I bite my lower lip. I most definitely did *not* want to see Rumplelawn. Even now that I've been there and seen it firsthand, I still wouldn't recommend it to a friend.

"Sure," I lie. "I mean, I've always been curious what the whole forest looks like, you know?" That part's true.

"Okay," Judder says. "Yer choice, not mine's. But, ifs ya don't minds, I'm 'a gonna waits outsides da town fer ya."

"Why?" I ask.

"Ummm. No reason."

I wonder if my lie sounded as obvious as his. I don't push it, though.

I slide down Judder's arm and he lowers me to the ground. I swear, even the moss here is softer than anywhere else. I lick my palm and run my hand through my hair, as if that'll do anything to help tame my treads. My heart's thumping like it wants to break free from my chest. This is the moment I've been waiting for my whole life. No pressure. I take a deep breath, give Judder a quick thumbs up, then march through the shimmering trees of Plethora.

Inside the village, glorious spider webs stretch from branch to branch, holding the morning dew and reflecting the sunlight in little tiny rainbows. So that's how they get the glittering effect in their trees. The flowers peppered along the ground are just as vibrant and evenly spaced. My eyes are completely overwhelmed by all the color and symmetry here. It's just like how I've imagined it!

"Oh. Em. Gee!" A nasal voice chirps from my left.

I turn to look and can't keep my mouth from flopping open at the sight. The elf standing before me is tall, but not as tall as I pictured. Maybe three quarters of a broom in height. *My disguise stilts would have made me too tall*, I can't help but think. Her hair cascades off her shoulders and well past her waist. It's yellow and so luminous, I bet it even glows in the dark.

"Wow," I squeal. I can't help myself. "I am your biggest fan."

The blomalfur just stares at me with her enormous diamond eyes that match her elaborate floral dress perfectly. I knew they must have cool clothes!

"Who, or rather what, are you?" she asks in that same nasal voice.

"Oh…uh…well…" I'm suddenly tongue-tied. And starstruck.

"Oh dear," she murmurs, a hint of disgust entering her voice. "I hope this isn't the start of another rodent infestation."

"No!" I shout. "No, nothing like that. I'm a trealfur elf. We're practically cousins! In fact, I'm pretty sure there was a mistake when I was born. I think I was supposed to be one of you…" I can't stop rambling. "I'm your biggest fan," I say again.

"Ugh," the blomalfur rolls her sparkling eyes. "I do not have time for this again."

"Again?" I'm confused. "But, this is my first time here. I mean, at least in real life. I've been here tons in my dreams, of course…"

"Basil!" the willowy elf calls.

Another equally gorgeous blomalfur strides elegantly into view.

"Yes, Amethyst?" he lulls in a voice even more nasal than his friends, if that's possible.

"We really need to build up our walls," Amethyst, with the glowing hair, sighs. "These adoring fans from the outside just won't leave us alone."

"Well, can you blame them?" the elf called Basil says. "It's a wonder the entire forest isn't spying on us nonstop." He pats his bright green hair as he speaks, arm muscles bulging with the movement.

I blush. Other huldufolk spy on Plethora, too?

"I must say," Basil continues, turning his back to me as if I don't even exist. "Your hair's looking ravishing today, boo. You look even smarter than usual, not like that's actually possible."

Amethyst smiles and twirls a piece of her yellow locks in her finger.

"And what about mine?" Basil asks. "Doesn't mine look simply divine as well?"

"Ahem!" I cough into my hand to get their attention. No luck. "AHEM!" I try again, even louder.

Basil turns around and looks down at me.

"What in mercy's name is that?" he gasps.

"This is what I'm talking about," Amethyst says, pointing right at me. "This little pest just traipsed right in here, babbling on and on about how it wishes it *was* me. Can you imagine?"

"Ewww!" Basil places his hand on his bare chest

like he's just been terribly offended. "It's absolutely hideous! How gross for you! Like anything that tiny could ever have a brain like yours."

"Right?" Amethyst agrees.

Even though I'm already smaller than these two elves anyway, I suddenly feel like the most insignificant thing in the entire forest.

"Do you think we could smash it?" Basil asks.

"And get its guts all over my feet? No thank you." Amethyst scoffs.

I get the hint. I am not welcome here. I turn and run back out of the perfectly symmetrical trees without even saying goodbye. Not that they notice me leave anyway. For the first time in my entire life, I want absolutely nothing to do with Plethora.

CHAPTER SEVENTEEN

Judder and I journey on past Plethora and back into the thick of the Bungaborg Forest. He doesn't ask a single question about my time in the blomalfur village, but I can tell from our mutual looks of disgust that he's had the exact same experience with those self-centered elves. No wonder he didn't want to go in there.

"Alrighty," he says after several more paces. "We's gotsta goes to da engi now ta find da base of da volcano."

"Right," I say, glad we finally get to act on my idea to be in the wide-open engi. "But first, I'm starving. Let's stop for a little snack." I spot a bush peppered with the most unusual purple berries.

I pluck one of the fruits off the bush. It's shaped like the sliver of the moon. It's beautiful.

I lift the berry up to my lips, but before I can stick it in my mouth, Judder leaps toward me and swats it away.

"You's can not eats anythin' you's wants out here," he scolds, scooping me quickly up into his hand where I can't touch anything. "Dems berries'll poisons ya in two seconds flat."

Yikes. I wrap my hands together behind my back. Lesson learned.

A rustle in the leaves startles us both. What was that? My heart thumps and I crouch down, trying to hide behind Judder's shoulder.

Creek. Snap! The branches move again. I'm pretty sure even Judder can hear my heartbeat now.

"Um, Judder?" I whisper. "Are there any, you know, scary creatures living in the faery ring?"

Judder's head nods up and down.

"Course," he says matter-of-factly, as if I just asked him if he breaths oxygen or something.

Rustle, rustle.

"...and, should we be worried about those types of things right now?"

"Course," he says again. He turns his head to

face me. "Didn't ya know dat 'fore we started dis whole journey?"

I gulp. I guess I should've asked more questions before we left Rumplelawn. I just assumed all the scary things wandered around the engi and Dreki Mountain. I know, I know, call me naive.

Crackle. THUMP!

We both jerk our heads in the direction of the sound. A fluffy gray rabbit is sitting there, staring us down with his beady black eyes. My heart leaps in relief.

Wait a minute, I've seen this rodent before. It's the same animal I saw in the engi yesterday! The one with the black ear. I guess the falcon didn't scoop him up for a snack after all.

"C'mon, Judder, let's keep moving." I turn my glance away from the animal and say into the troll's ear.

Judder keeps looking at the rabbit.

"Why's id jus' starin' ad us like dat?" he asks. He doesn't sound so much annoyed as curious.

"Don't know, don't care," I say. I've never been terribly fond of rabbits. Too fuzzy.

Judder shrugs, then faces forward and starts walking again. The rabbit hops right in front of our path.

"Get out of the way!" I call. "Or, we'll run you over."

"No's we won'ts," Judder sighs and pats my head.

I growl.

The bunny just stares at us.

"I think he's tryin' ta tells us somethin,'" Judder suggests.

The rabbit twitches his little pink nose.

"Whaddya need, 'iddle friend?" Judder leans over to ask.

My cheeks burn to hear him call this pest the same nickname he calls me. I look down. The rabbit looks up. We glare at each other for a good long time, just daring the other to be the first to blink. I don't know how I ended up in a staring contest with a puffball of a rabbit, but here we are.

"I wish me's could talk ta animals," Judder says, breaking the tension.

His comment makes me think of Aspen. I smile at the thought.

"My brother can communicate with animals," I say proudly. "I wish Aspen was here."

The rabbit's ears perk up at the sound of my brother's name. He hops into action, pointing his paws back toward the direction we came from and chittering away like it's something really, really urgent. What in the world?

"Aspen?" I say the word again.

The rabbit freaks out even more, kicking his hind legs into the ground and pushing up a cloud of dust.

"Iz somethin' wrongs wiff Aspen?" Judder asks.

The rabbit just keeps kicking and pointing back toward Rumplelawn.

I panic. Is Aspen really in trouble?

"We have to go back," I blurt.

Judder jerks his neck to look at me.

"Really?"

"Yes, really," I say. "If something's wrong with Aspen, I need to help him. That's way more important than finding the dreki."

"Okays," Judder says. "If you's says so."

He picks one foot up, then the other, and turns

to face the direction we can from. I secure my balance on his shoulder and we start retracing our steps. The rabbit leads the way, sprinting quickly between trees and brush. Every so often, he turns around to see if we're still following him. We are, but Judder can't keep up with his clunky feet. He certainly can't move in and out of branches like the rodent can. The rabbit looks distraught. Or maybe he's annoyed. I can't quite tell. Either way, it's clear we're not moving fast enough for the rabbit's liking. Something must be terribly wrong with Aspen.

"Is there a quicker way?" I ask Judder.

He shakes his head. "Not dat I knows of. At least not unless you's can ride ons an animal er somethin'."

I whistle to the rabbit. He stops and looks at me with his beady eyes. I really don't like when he does that. I close my own eyes and picture the way Aspen would approach an animal he wanted to ride. He'd do it full of total trust and respect. Too bad I don't feel an ounce of either of those things for this rabbit. Not to mention, there's no way he could carry my weight that far. That thing isn't even twice as big as me. Still, I don't think I have much time to find another option.

I slide down Judder's arm and he lowers me onto the ground. I reach my hand out hoping it comes across as some sort of sign of peace. The rabbit twitches his nose.

"Can I ride with you?" I ask, even though I know he can't understand a word I'm saying.

I take another step toward him. He doesn't move. That's a good sign. I reach his gray fur and stroke his back, like I've seen Aspen do dozens of times. The rabbit lets out a contented whimper. I put both my hands on his back and try to mount the thing. He squeals and scampers away from me. *Ooof!* I land face first on the ground. So much for that idea. But, the rabbit doesn't leave us. Instead, he hops toward me again, then lifts his head up toward the sky and makes the strangest sound I've ever heard.

YEEEEEEAAAAARRRRP!

Judder and I both cover our ears. What in the world was that? The rabbit does it two more times.

The bushes around us start trembling. Great, now we're all going to get eaten by a scary creature. But, a scary creature isn't what emerges. Instead, it's another rabbit. This one looks slightly less fluffy than the first, but not by much. The two rodents arrange themselves side-by-side, then the black-eared one looks at me with its beady eyes and motions me over with his head.

I look back to Judder for guidance, but he just shrugs, which is of no help whatsoever.

"All right," I throw my hands up in the air. "Let's try this out."

I walk in the space between the two rabbits and place a hand on each of their backs. When they don't run away from me, I pull myself up and plant a foot on each critter. They nod their approval. Standing straight up on two rodents' backs doesn't seem like the safest idea in the world, but before I have time to mention that, they take off running perfectly in sync. Who knew they could do that?

"I'll follow you's and meets ya back there!" Judder calls out as we race ahead, back toward Rumplelawn.

CHAPTER EIGHTEEN

I make it back to Rumplelawn in no time flat thanks to my rabbit ride. They slow down right in front of Judder's family cave.

"Aspen's in there?" I ask, jumping off the rabbits.

No one answers me.

An ear-smashing squeal comes out of the front entrance of the cave, though.

"AIEEEEEEE!!!!!" a female's voice screams. "WHAD'S A TREALFUR DOIN' IN ME'S HOUSE!!!"

I run into the cave to find a troll even bigger than Judder standing inside. She looks mad. Really mad. On the ground, a cage made out of dry sticks covers something. Or rather, someone. Aspen!

I feel sick to my stomach. A sudden thumping

sound of footsteps at the cave entrance behind me tells me there's more than one troll in this whole nightmare. The thought of it only makes me feel more ill. The woman troll clearly hears them, too. She looks up and her face softens immediately.

"Me boy!" she cries in a low, raspy voice, her scowl disappearing completely.

"Hey, ma," I hear Judder's voice.

I let out a breath I didn't realize I was holding in. I scamper backward and hide behind my friend's legs.

"Where've you's been, son?" The female troll walks right over to him and gives his cheeks a pat, seemingly forgetting all about the trapped trealfur in the middle of her family room.

I keep myself hidden, just so she doesn't have the opportunity to catch two trealfurs in one day.

"I wuz jus' out an' about," Judder shrugs. He's a terrible liar. Luckily, his mom doesn't seem to notice one bit.

"Dat's nice," she says, that smile still beaming on her face.

"Maybe you's can helps me wit' somethin' if

dat's okay?" She asks sweetly enough.

"Course!" Judder answers quickly. I'm sure he'd do anything to keep his mom from remembering about the cage.

"Great!" She claps her hands together, making my ears ring. "Ya sees, I've gots me dis 'iddle pest problem it seems." She points to the caged Aspen.

So much for forgetting about the trealfur in the middle of the room.

"Ain't nobody wantin' no trealfurs 'round here, amiright, son? I hears dem's are all full's of fleas and stuff from stayin' trapped up in dat town's of ders. Can you's please gets me a rock? I'm 'a gonna smash dis thing till it's a bootiful, gooey puddle."

I clap both my hands over my mouth to keep from screaming. Judder shifts from one foot to the other while his mom waits for an answer. Before he can say anything, that blasted rabbit with the black ear leaps through the doorway and scampers over to Judder's side.

Judder's mom's eyes shift from Judder down to the rodent and grow wide with panic. She screams, then reaches down and lifts the cage off Aspen in order to try to catch the rabbit. Aspen scrambles quickly away, but instead of running toward freedom, he barrels right into Judder's leg. Even though Aspen's tiny compared to the troll, he clearly catches Judder off guard. The troll jumps in surprise, shifting his feet just enough to leave me totally and completely exposed. Judder's mom and I lock eyes for a split second before she lunges right at me. I run. I can't think clearly enough to figure out where I should run to though, so I end up sprinting around the indoor perimeter of Judder's family cave in circles.

The rabbit seems to think this is all a game, because he starts chasing me—that blasted thing. Aspen joins in the chaos and starts running behind the rabbit. Judder's mom falls in line behind Aspen, jogging rather slowly to stay behind us and holding the cage up high above her head, ready to snap it down at just the right moment. Judder takes up the rear, trying to grab the cage from his mom's hand. And so it continues. All of us in a bizarre little parade, chasing each other around and around in circles in a troll's cave. Who knows how long the whole thing goes on, but I'm definitely getting dizzy. No way am I stopping, though. All that talk about rocks and gooey puddles? No thank you.

"WUT'S GOIN' ON IN HEEEERE?!" Yet another voice booms. It's clear this one belongs to a male troll. A very angry male troll.

We all stop, even the rabbit. This new, even bigger troll is standing in the cave's entrance, looking sternly from Judder to Judder's mom.

"WILL SOMEONE EXPLAIN'S DIS TO ME'S, PLEASE!" It's a demand, not a question.

"Sweetheart," Judder's mom shuffles over to the larger troll.

"I'm sooo glad yer home's," Judder's mom says. "We've gots 'a real pest problem we do. Quick, gets some rocks!!"

But Judder's dad doesn't have time to get even one smashing tool before Judder takes a step forward, putting himself in between his parents and me.

"NOOO!" Judder yells almost as loudly as his dad. I had no idea he was capable of sounding like that.

Apparently, his parents had no idea either, because they both look at him with total shock plastered across their faces.

"ENUFF!" Judder bellows again now that he has everyone's full attention. "I've had me's enuff of alls of dis. Jus' 'cause these 'iddle guys are trealfurs, it doesn't mean them's got rabies or somethin'."

My lip quivers slightly. No one's ever stood up for me like this before.

Judder keeps going. "An' jus' 'cause I'm's an troll, doesn't mean I can't likes 'um. Everyone thinks we've gots ta act a certain way an' stick ta our owns people. But, we don't. These guys is so nice. An' they ain'ts pests. Tinsey's me best friend!"

I bite the insides of my cheeks to keep from smiling too much. I'm his best friend? Even though I'm standing in a cave about to be smashed by some angry trolls, this is the happiest moment of my entire life.

CHAPTER NINETEEN

"Dem's yer friends?" Judder's dad looks stunned.

Judder nods once, then folds his arms across his chest, letting his parents know he's not about to back down. His dad purses his lips—or at least purses where his lips would be if he had any—then loosens them and lets out a low whistle.

"Interestin'," he says. After a quick pause, he shrugs and says, "Welp, sorry to say son, but dat's jus' not okay." He turns toward his wife. "Sweetheart, goes an' gets me them's rocks."

Judder gasps. I shudder. The rabbit lifts up his hind leg and scratches an itch behind his ear. But Judder's mom doesn't budge.

"Sweetheart," Judder's dad says again.

His mom looks at Judder. Then her eyes flick toward Aspen and me in an almost apologetic glance before shuffling out of the cave. She comes back in with an armful of rocks, but her face doesn't look at all certain of what's about to happen. Isn't it strange that she was the one who originally wanted to smash us all? Now, it almost seems like she's second guessing the whole thing. Maybe there's a way to convince her to let us live.

"Your son's a really great chef!" I yell.

Everyone stops and stares down at me. *Be brave*, I tell myself.

"Seriously," I continue in the strongest voice I can muster. "He makes the best food I've ever eaten in my entire life. How could I have known that if I hadn't met him? Imagine all the amazing trealfurs out there with all sorts of cool talents and whatever that the rest of the forest doesn't even know about. You can't judge us all because of a decision we have no control over!"

I have to admit, it's not a great argument, but it's all I can come up with in a pinch. Luckily, it seems to work. Judder's mom lowers the rocks slightly and twists her mouth up.

"You's really think's it wuz da best food you's ever hads?" she asks quietly.

I nod. "The absolute best!"

That makes her smile.

"Thanks fer sayin' dat," she says to me.

I smile up at her.

"DIS IZ RIDICULOUS!" Judder's dad ruins the moment from his corner of the cave. "YOU'S GETTIN' BRAINWASHED BY DAT PEST! MAYBE IT GAVE YOU ID'S RAIBIES!!"

He runs forward and grabs a rock from his wife's arms, then lifts it above his head and aims right at Aspen. Aspen jumps out of the way just in time, but Judder's dad is already working on reloading. Without thinking, I snap my fingers together twice. Two giant brooms appear on either side of Judder's dad and start sweeping the ground at his feet. He gets tangled up in them and wobbles, swinging his arms in circles and trying to regain his balance.

"WHOAAAAAA!" he cries just before crashing face first onto the ground.

"Come on!" I yell.

Everyone jumps over Judder's dad and runs to freedom, even Judder. Everyone, that is, except for me. My legs feel even weaker than usual before they give out and I collapse to the ground. Judder's mom lunges toward me. I cover my head with my arms, as if that's going to give me any sort of protection. But, the blow never comes. Instead, I feel my wobbly body get scooped up by a pair of sweaty hands. Like Judder's, only the stench is slightly different.

"Bee's careful, 'iddle friend," the female troll whispers in my ear. "An', takes cares of me son."

I look up from her palms just in time to notice a little twinkle in her eye. She runs out of the cave and passes me over to Judder.

"I loves you's!" she sings to him.

Judder blushes, and there's no hiding the giant grin on his face. He scoops up Aspen and sets him on the opposite shoulder from me. Together, we run back into the thick of the forest. Once we've got a good cadence going, I feel brave enough to stand up on Judder and walk over to my brother. It's time for some answers. I sit down next to Aspen and start right in.

"What in the world is going on?" I ask.

"Fair enough," Aspen says simply. "First thing's first, the rabbit's name is Sky."

"I didn't ask about the blasted rabbit!" I growl. "I don't care about that pesky thing."

"Fine," Aspen says. "But, he's an integral part of this whole explanation. Now, if you'll let me continue."

I close my mouth and silently promise to keep my thoughts to myself.

"I met Sky yesterday afternoon," Aspen continues. "After you came out from behind that tree wearing your ridiculous costume, I knew I couldn't do anything to stop you from trying to go to Plethora. So, I found the first animal I could and made friends with that little guy." He motions backward with his thumb. Sky's sprinting behind us, his puffball body bouncing off the ground. "I asked Sky to follow you. You know, just to keep an eye on you. To make sure you didn't get into any trouble."

"So, Sky's a spy?"

It's too ridiculous a thought. There's no way

that fluffy rodent is capable of snooping around. Then again, that rabbit did track me down in the middle of the faery ring. He also knew exactly what to do when my brother was in trouble. Maybe he's not so bad after all.

So, Sky must have followed the falcon through the engi and saw that I didn't end up in Plethora. He knew I went with Judder to his cave for dinner, then stayed the night in Rumplelawn.

"But wait..." I say. One thing doesn't make sense. "How did you end up in Judder's house?"

Aspen nods, like he was expecting that question.

"Sky came back to Snugglepunk late last night and told me about the dreki you guys saw. How that monster lit up our trees. I won't lie, that made me nervous, Tins. Like, really nervous. I couldn't just sit back and wait for you to make your way home knowing there's a dragon on the prowl."

"So you came over to Judder's house to try to protect me?" I guess.

"Exactly. But, you guys had already left when I got there. That's when I met Judder's charming mom." His sarcasm is loud and clear.

Judder hears Aspen's comment, too, but the sarcasm falls flat on him.

"My mom is charming, rights?" He beams.

I stifle a laugh.

So, Sky must have seen Judder's mom trap Aspen, then came to find me.

The leaves around us start to shake again. Perfect timing! I can't wait to say thanks to Sky's little buddy who helped carry me back to Rumplelawn. A paw steps into view through the brush. A very large paw. It most definitely does not belong to a rabbit.

CHAPTER TWENTY

The thick paw settles firmly on the ground, followed by its companion. The coat on this creature is a strange burnt orange color I've never seen on an animal. Two front legs come into view. Chunks of fur are missing, leaving the pink, shriveled skin beneath exposed. The second its wet, black snout presses out of the brush, Judder leaps backward.

"Close yer eyes an' don't moves a muscle!" he yells.

Aspen and I both obey.

"It's a skoffin fox," Judder says quietly. "One's of da mos' dangerous critters out here's."

Great. So much for making it to my twelfth birthday.

I can hear the vines shift as the animal makes its

way completely through them. Its paws pad softly on the ground, like it's on a prowl. I swear I feel my stomach sink down to my toes. This thing is hunting us.

"Can we open our eyes?" I ask, although I'm not sure I actually want to see what's going on. Maybe being blind to it all is better.

"Absolutely nots!" Judder warns in a stern voice. "Skoffin's can kills ya jus' by lookin' you's straights in da eyes."

Okay then, I will definitely not be opening my eyes.

We stand in silence listening for the beast. I brace myself and wait for it to attack us. But, it doesn't. In fact, I can't even hear it walking anymore.

"Is it still there?" I ask.

"I'm sure's of it," Judder responds. "It's jus' waitin' fer us to takes a peek."

I hear the same soft padding sound to my right. Is that another skoffin? More pattering to my left. And twice as much behind me. I lick my lips and gulp hard with the realization that these things are surrounding us.

"Why aren't they fighting us?" Aspen asks in a harsh whisper.

His voice in my ear makes my entire body feel warm. At least he's next to me.

"Oh, them's won' make da first move. They're waitin' fer us to move first."

So, at least we have that going for us, right?

"They don't gives up easy, though. Them's been known ta wait fer there prey ta move or's opens its eyes fer days. Eventually's, da prey can' take it no more and falls overs an' dies of starvation or whatevers."

Thanks for the words of encouragement, Judder, I think.

"So, what do we do?" Aspen asks.

"Nuttin'," Judder says quietly.

"But, we've got to do something," I say. We can't just stand here for days and days until we collapse. "Haven't you seen one of these in the forest before, Judder? What did you do then?"

"I ain'ts never seens one. They're super rare's. I jus' know da color of their fur cause we's learn 'bout how dangerous they are when we's jus' tiny babies."

I try to picture the creatures with their missing fur in my mind. From the bits I saw, I'm imagining them looking almost foxlike. I picture their eyes, glowing red and shooting rays of poison out of them. There's got to be a way to stop that from happening. A way to clean up their death stares.

Clean!

Maybe I could drum up a tool that could help us. Would the skoffins notice the movement if I snapped my fingers together? What I wouldn't give for a water basin like the one I created yesterday. It could temporarily blind the skoffins with its lemony cleaning solution. Except, that probably wouldn't happen. I mean, what if something wonky comes in instead and ruins the whole situation? I think of the broom that swept through the entire trealfur council circle and made everyone move out of the way. Something that would force us to move? That would definitely be a bad thing right now. And, since brooms seem to be my most common thing, I guess I shouldn't risk it. Of course, spending days just standing here doesn't sound like a great alternative.

"Aspen," I say.

"Yeah?"

"What kind of animal do you think you can call over right now?"

"Well, any type I guess, but…" he pauses. "Wouldn't a skoffin just kill anything with eyes?"

Right.

Wait a minute. "We have eyes and the skoffins haven't killed us yet," I point out. "So, it won't kill anything with *eyes*. It will kill anything with *sight*. Do you think there are any moles around? They're blind, right?"

"Yes, they are," Aspen answers. "And rather aggressive."

"Perfect. I'll distract the skoffins with my magic, then you call some moles over to help us out, okay?"

Aspen doesn't answer.

"What's wrong?" I ask.

"Well, no offense, Tins," he responds, "but…can you control your magic?"

This time, I'm the one who doesn't answer. I've got to try to control it. There's no other choice. I picture Mom and Dad sitting at home in our cave, wondering where their kids are. How awful for them to find out they've lost both children in one attack. A puddle of tears presses against my closed eyelids at the thought. I've got to make this work. If not for us, then for them. More tears pool when I remember how my last interaction with my parents was me screaming at them for not understanding me. What was I thinking? Of course they understand me. Better than those lousy blomalfur elves I thought I'd fit in with so well. A warmth starts to fill my heart just thinking about Mom and Dad. Mom's music, Dad's laugh. I'll never hear those things again. The warmth spreads from my heart to my arm, moving quickly down toward my fingers. Without any active help from me, my thumb and forefinger push together and snap.

Splash. Splash.

The smell of lemons fills my nostrils. Did I really just conjure up a wooden basin? On purpose?

The skoffins start yelping in pain. I picture the bowls splashing right into their poisonous eyes.

"Call the moles!" I yell over the sound of the howls toward Aspen.

He clicks his tongue and makes some snarling noises. Sure enough, what sounds like an army of tiny pattering paws is pure music to my ears. Growls fill the air, following by some snarls and a handful of high-pitched yips.

I have no idea what's going on. I can't stand it any longer. I open one eye to take a peek.

CHAPTER TWENTY-ONE

Sparkling wooden tubs are flying around, splashing as they go. Dozens of small, gray moles are jumping through the air, teeth bared and ready to attack. They're landing on the backs of five disgusting looking foxes. Each skoffin's dirty orange fur is matted and poorly patched. Even in its thickest parts, it's practically hanging off the skoffins' skinny bodies. I can tell their eyes are huge even though they're all squinting shut from the surprise of the lemon water.

"Look!" I call to my friends.

Judder and Aspen both open their eyes and look down at the chaos happening at our feet.

"Whoa," Aspen gives a low whistle.

I notice the smallest of the skoffins. It seems more composed than the others and is aggressively batting at its eyes with its paws, like it's trying to figure out how to regain visibility. I can't imagine we have much time before the shock from the splashing water wears off for them all.

"Come on!" I scream over the raucous. "We've got to get out of here."

I stand up on Judder's shoulder in excitement.

"Like, now!" I scream again.

Judder nods and starts running. I try to sit back down on his shoulder, but my legs do that wobbly thing they always do after I use my magic. I lose my balance and topple off Judder, hardly even having enough energy to flail as I fall down to the ground. Judder doesn't notice. He keeps running.

My head throbs and my vision's blurry, but I can at least make out the shapes of the skoffins and moles ahead of me. The basins are gone. An orangey blob that must be one of the skoffins lifts its head and twitches its ears. I hold my breath. The picture grows clearer just in time for me to watch the skoffin sniff the ground and turn its head in my direction.

Oh no. I shut my eyes tight and curl up in a ball

on the ground, trying to stay perfectly still. Maybe it didn't see me. Maybe it's just checking out its surroundings. I know better. I hear those same padding footsteps getting closer and closer. I feel a wet snout on the top of my head. I beg myself not to scream.

YEEEEEEAAAAARRRRP!

Did that come out of my mouth? No, it couldn't have. My lips are sealed up so tight. I've heard that high-pitched cry before, though.

YEEEEEEAAAAARRRRP! It calls again.

In an instant, I know. It's Sky the rabbit spy! I feel the rabbit's soft fur press against me, then he pushes under me and lifts me up onto his back. He darts off and takes a quick right into a hole in the vines. I fly off his back and roll into the warm heather. We're safe!

"Thanks, Sky!" I cheer, standing up and dusting myself off. "That was incredible!"

But, Sky's nowhere to be found.

"Sky?" I look around.

He couldn't have gotten far. He was right here with me. I look toward the vines we came through.

On the ground, a tiny gray puff of a tail lays motionless.

"Sky!" I scream, running to him.

I pull the rest of his body into the safety of the vines. He's completely limp. His eyes are shut tight. I cradle him in my arms and stroke his one black ear.

I can't stop the tears from coming. Sky risked his life to save mine. He caught the skoffin's stare so I wouldn't have to. I sob big, sloppy tears. It's not fair. It's just not fair.

"Tinsey?" I hear Aspen's voice. It sounds like it's way off in the distance, but then I feel his hand on my shoulder. "I'm sorry, Tins," he says softly.

"Did you call Sky and ask him to do that?" I turn and look at my brother.

He shakes his head and looks a little guilty.

"I didn't even think to do that. It was all him. I didn't help at all, Tins. I'm so sorry."

I cry even harder.

"Do you want to go home now?" Aspen asks gently.

I shake my head firmly. No.

"We need to get to Dreki Mountain," I say. "For Sky. We need to finish this."

"But, Tins…" Aspen trails off.

I know what he wants to say.

"I know the dreki might kill us," I say. "Of course I know that. But, I need to get that stone back and make things right."

Aspen sits up straight and nods his head once.

"Okay," he says. "If you're still in, then I'm in, too. For Sky."

"For Sky," I repeat, throwing my arms around my big brother and squeezing him as tightly as I possibly can.

Aspen starts humming a tune we sing whenever a trealfur dies. It's slow and sad-sounding. I join in, matching his pitch as best I can. He pats my hair and holds me close as we sing our goodbyes to Sky.

The bunny's gray fur shifts with the soft breeze, like it's dancing to our song. For a second, it looks like Sky's front paw even twitches a bit, joining in. If only. And then, I see it again. Are my eyes just playing tricks on me? I stop singing and tug at Aspen's hand.

"Look!" I whisper and point at Sky's paw.

Now, Sky's back leg jerks. Aspen rubs his eyes, like he's just as confused as me.

"Sky?" He asks timidly.

The bunny flutters his eyes open and shut a couple times, then looks up at Aspen without lifting his head off the ground.

I can't believe it! He's alive!

CHAPTER TWENTY-TWO

"Sky!" I scream, not even trying to hide my joy. He didn't catch a skoffin's stare after all! "Oh, Sky! I'm so happy!"

Of course, the bunny can't understand a word I'm saying. He just stares at me with his little beady eyes. He blinks a couple of times, pushes himself up onto his legs and wiggles his rear end back and forth a bit, like he's shaking off what just happened. He twitches his nose once. Twice. Then, he scampers away. Just like that. No goodbyes, no *thank you for that beautiful song, guys.* I smile anyway. After all, that little guy saved my life.

"Hey guys," Judder pants, running into view from behind the brush.

To be honest, I didn't even realize he wasn't

with us this whole time. Not like I would ever say that to him, though.

"Wut did I's miss?" He asks.

Oh boy. Where to even start?

Aspen clears his throat.

"Uh, not much," he says.

Judder nods, like he's totally fooled.

"Okay guys," I say, feeling done with this awkward little exchange. "We've got a long journey ahead of us. Let's go get our family's stone back."

"Um, Tinsey?" Judder says.

"Yeah?"

"We's closer dan you's thinks."

He steps through the vines and onto the outskirts of the engi, then points straight up. I follow and take a look. Dreki Mountain! It's right in front of us. And, it's huge. Even when I crane my neck as far back as it'll go, I still can't see the top. There's no way we can climb this thing on our own. Aspen must have had the same thought, because he looks toward me and asks, "Are you thinking what I'm thinking?"

I'm pretty sure I am.

"Caw! Caw!" Aspen chirps into the sky.

I close my eyes and picture Sky helping me out. The same warmth I felt earlier runs from my heart, down my arm, and into my fingers. I snap, and when I open my eyes, an enormous wooden-handled mop appears in the air and clatters to the ground next to me. Perfect! Judder and I get to work untying the thick, braided vines on the mop head, which unravel easily into one flat rope of sorts. I do some quick calculations: this rope seems to be roughly fifty feet long. The volcano must be 13,000 feet tall. That's two hundred and sixty ropes high. A couple of the sparrows Aspen summoned pick up one end of the cord and fly it up as high as it will go on the rigid side of the volcano, then peck it into a tight hold in the rocks. The other birds position themselves along the rope's course, holding it in place with their talons.

I tug at the braid of vines from the bottom. When it doesn't shift, I hand it to Judder. He tries it. Even with his strength, it stays surprisingly secure. Nice work, birds! Aspen and I climb up to

Judder's shoulders and Judder heaves himself onto the first stretch of the mountain. He uses the rope sparingly, just to keep his balance while he's scrambling up the rocks.

When we make it to the top of the rope, the birds loosen it from its wedge in the rocks and lift it up to its highest reach. Two-hundred-and-fifty-nine laps to go.

Up, up, up we go. Every push of Judder's legs makes me lose my breath just a little bit more.

"There's less oxygen on top of a mountain, so it's harder to breath," Aspen says matter-of-factly. How does he know all this stuff?

The higher we go, it seems it's not just oxygen we're losing, it's visibility. The fog comes on slowly at first, spreading across the ground, then more quickly as it stretches its wispy arms upward, filling the air around us. By the time we reach the top, Judder looks like he's ready to collapse. I can't blame him.

The fog is thick and gray, and the ground beneath it is covered in black ash. The rocks up here look like they've been turned to molten more than once. I'm sure they have. Then there's the actual mouth of the volcano itself. A vast hole filled to the brim with bubbling red and orange lava puffs angrily. Creepy.

There's no turning back now, though. That much is clear. This whole thing was my idea. If I wimp out, that'd just be a punk move. So, I put on my strong face. My brave face. My let's-do-this-already face.

And then I see the dreki's lair behind the mouth of the volcano. It's enormous. Like, big enough to maybe even fit the entire engi inside of it. The edges are singed a dark, charcoal color.

I try not to think about how I could very well end up more toasted than those edges. At least I have someone really smart like Aspen and someone big and strong like Judder here with me.

"I'ms a 'iddle scared," Judder whispers through the fog.

"Yeah, me too," Aspen agrees with a low whistle.

Great, so much for counting on them to be courageous. I guess it's up to me, then.

I march past the volcano hole and up to the entrance of the cave.

"Hello?" I call inside.

No answer. It seems the dragon isn't home, which is great news. Now I can search for the gemstone without having to worry about anyone lighting me on fire.

I step inside and breathe in a strong whiff of stale smoke. That's not the surprising part. Not at all. In fact, I think I'd be more shocked if a dragon's home didn't smell like smoke. The thing that does surprise me is what I see in the far corner. A giant rocking chair made entirely out of tree trunks and branches is decorated in what seems to be a homemade afghan. Similar-looking blankets and quilts, all made with muted reds, blues, and greens, are flung around on the ground and draped on jutted rocks in the walls. Does the dragon knit? Did she build that furniture? I close my eyes and try to picture that enormous beast acting domestic in her giant rocking chair, moving a pair of knitting needles to and fro. Ridiculous.

Judder and Aspen appear beside me, apparently finding their own courage now that I've paved the way.

"Whoa," Aspen whispers. "It looks way less scary on the inside."

I have to agree. In fact, it looks downright cozy in here with all these quilts everywhere.

We all walk farther into the cave.

Aspen's hunting for the stone in what seems to be the dragon's kitchen, picking up random bits of leaves and berries strewn about.

Judder doesn't even pretend to search for anything. He makes his way straight over to the rocking chair and takes a seat. Without a second thought, he picks up an enormous pair of knitting needles and a ball of soft blue yarn that's lying on the ground, and starts working the wool around the needles.

"You can knit?" I ask, total shock dripping off my words.

"Sure," Judder says simply. "Can't you's?"

I shake my head.

"It's really not so hards," he shrugs.

I have to say, watching a troll sitting cross-legged in a giant rocking chair and knitting is a rather strange visual.

"With all these sheeps 'round," he continues, "it's easy's ta make da yarns. Lots of berries and stuff ta dye its with, too."

I feel totally cheated. How come no one ever taught me to knit? To think, I could have a whole wardrobe of colorful clothing!

"Where did all these fruits and veggies come from?" Aspen asks from the kitchen.

"Da garden!" Judder sings.

"The dreki has a garden?" Aspen and I ask at the same time.

"Oh yeah!" Judder says. "It's suppose' ta bee da mos' bootiful garden in alls of Bungabor…"

Before he can finish his sentence, a blast of smoke pushes through the front door and fills the space. I can hardly see a thing through the black soot, but I can definitely make out one thing as it smashes through the smoke. If I'm not mistaken, it looks an awful lot like a giant, purple claw.

CHAPTER TWENTY-THREE

There's a real-life dragon in the same space as us. Correction: a very angry real-life dragon. I do some quick math. If I'm a twelfth the size of Judder, and this dragon is at very least five times the height of my troll friend, that means she's twelve times five my size. Can you imagine? An angry beast sixty times larger than I am is blocking the only way out of this place. We're trapped! Judder and Aspen are both frozen stiff, Judder with the pair of enormous knitting needles in his hands, and Aspen holding a bushel of beets. Their jaws are hanging open. Mine wants to do the same thing, but I don't let it. No way am I gonna let this dreki know just how terrified I am.

The dreki stomps closer, causing a tiny earthquake with every step. Even with that nasty look on her face, she somehow still looks majestic. Shimmering purple scales, each one as large as me, ripple with even the smallest movement, making it seem like she's glowing. Triangular spikes matching the iridescent blue of her belly cascade from the top of her head all the way down her back and to the very tip of her thick, muscular tail. They're standing straight up like they're proud to be part of this magnificent creature's make up. I can't blame them; I'd be proud of that, too. The dreki's square snout blows puffs of smoke with every breath.

The most striking thing about this creature isn't her scales or her smoke or her tail, though. It's her eyes. They're almond-shaped and emerald green, almost exactly the same color as my own! While it's definitely pretty cool to know I have something in common with the Bungaborg Dreki, what really strikes me is how kind her eyes look. Even though she's clearly fuming, I can't help but wonder if maybe she's not such a bad egg. I mean, when you think about it, she just came home to find a bunch of small strangers inside her cave uninvited and messing with her stuff. I'd probably be blowing smoke out my nose if that happened to me, too.

"WHO ARE YOU AND WHY ARE YOU TRESPASSING HERE?!" she booms.

Or maybe I'm reading into this too much.

Judder drops the ball of yarn, which rolls across the floor. Aspen sets the beets down with a thud and backs away. Once more, it's up to me to fix things.

"Hello, Ms. Dragon." I use my biggest voice.

She looks down at me.

"Uh…" I try to find my words. I wasn't actually expecting this beast to hear me.

My brain goes completely blank. All I can think about is how quickly the smoke pouring out of her nose could turn into fire. It's one thing to talk to a thirty-foot dragon who isn't looking at you, but it's much harder when she's staring you down.

"Um…" I start again. "Ms. Dragon…Hi…Oh, um…My name's Tinsey Clover. It's very nice to meet you."

I extend my hand out to shake hers, which is ridiculous since mine's like the size of a pumpkin seed by comparison. She just glares at me. This is so not going well. On the other hand, at least she hasn't charred us to a crisp yet.

"YOU DIDN'T ANSWER MY QUESTION," she snarls. "WHY ARE YOU HERE?!"

"Listen," I say, trying to calm this monster down a bit. "I'm sorry we broke into your cave. That was very rude of us. And to be messing with your stuff? I'm beyond ashamed."

I glare at Judder, who releases his grip on the knitting needles. They clatter to the floor.

"But," I continue, "the thing is, I saw you steal something of mine. Well, my people's, I mean."

The dragon scoffs. "And what, pray tell, did you see me steal?" She still sounds furious, but at least she's not yelling anymore.

"Well," I start, suddenly feeling rather foolish to be accusing anything of a beast who's blowing smoke out her nose. "It was a large, light blue gemstone attached to the top of a tree. It belongs to my people. I saw you take it after you lit my town on fire yesterday…"

She reels back a bit at the mention of the

incident. We all sink down a little bit with fear.

"Anyway," I go on uncertainly, "I wonder if I might have it back. It means so much to my village. I know you'll probably just turn me to ashes right now, but I had to at least ask."

Luckily, the dragon doesn't do anything of the sort. Instead, her kind-looking green eyes start to glimmer with the potential for tears. Yes, tears! Can you even imagine how huge a dragon's tears must be? It looks like she's seconds away from crying now, which means we're all moments away from getting washed away in a flood of salt water.

CHAPTER TWENTY-FOUR

I have no idea what to do. I've never comforted a crying dreki before. Should I give her a hug? I don't know that it'd do much good given how my arms probably couldn't even wrap all the way around her pinkie talon.

"There, there," I pat her claw instead. I have no idea why people say "there, there" when they're trying to console someone else. It makes absolutely no sense. And yet, here I am, petting a shimmering purple scale and saying it.

A giant, runny drop of snot falls from the monster's huge nostril and lands right on top of my head, sliming up my hair and turning it more dark violet than purple. Gross. I try not to react, but it's really, really hard. I mean, I'm covered in dragon boogers!

"Sorry," the dragon mumbles.

I look up at her and force a smile. "No prob." I keep patting her claw.

The dragon sighs and starts in on her story.

"It's just, well you see, I've had this cold lately," she sobs. "Of course I've had colds before, but this one's been really bad. I can't sleep, I can't think straight. I can't even find the energy to knit, if you can believe that!"

I smile to show I'm listening. I'm still having a hard time believing a dragon can actually knit in the first place.

"Anyway," she continues in a voice that's just as majestic as the rest of her. "When I was a little dragonlet, my grandmother used to bring me this herb that could help cure colds. Magneosyde. It only grows on the other side of the forest, but way back then, it wasn't considered inappropriate to travel there. I really don't like to go into the faery ring these days, but this cold was really bothering me. I figured, what's the harm in flying there really quickly to pick a batch of Magneosyde, you know?"

I nod like I get it. In reality, I have no idea what any of this has to do with the Snugglepunk Safety Stone.

"So, I flew across the forest," the dreki continues. "Only, on my way back, I sneezed. Now, a sneeze to you might not be that big of a deal, but when a dragon sneezes, fire comes out. I can't help it, it's just what happens." She looks a little sheepish.

"Anyway, I wasn't paying much attention to where my flames landed, to be quite honest. I certainly can't control their direction when I sneeze. I flew back to my mountain straight away to fetch some water from the creek outside my garden."

Creek outside her garden? I seem to have missed a lot earlier. I guess her mountain isn't so barren after all.

"But, by the time I flew back to where I'd started the fire," she continues, "it was already extinguished. I must say, your people have a highly efficient way of putting out flames."

"But wait," Aspen interjects. "There's been

more than one fire in Snugglepunk this week. If you only went to get that herb once, how did the other fires start?"

"Yeah," I chime in, too. "And what about the gemstone? I know for a fact you took that."

The dragon looks downright embarrassed, like she's been caught in a lie.

"Well," she says timidly. "I didn't just go there once. I thought that's all it would take since that's all it took when I was a dragonlet."

I squint my eyes and try to imagine just how small a dragonlet might be. Probably still twenty times my size.

"But," she goes on, "when you're as big as I am now, it turns out you need a lot of Magneosyde to make any sort of a difference. So, even though I picked a whole clump the first time, it hardly lasted a full day. I had to get more. And, I don't know what it is about that section of the Bungaborg, but something near your town really tickles my throat. I sneeze at the exact same place every time. Maybe I've grown allergic to trealfurs in my old age." She shrugs.

I take a step back, just in case.

"Each time I'd light a fire," the dragon continues, "I'd panic and leave. Of course, I'd feel terrible and return, but every time I came back, the fire would be gone. Anyway," she sighs. "Last night, I noticed my flames getting awfully close to your people's treasured stone. I couldn't stand to watch that burn, so I took it away from the fire. I had full intention of returning it, I can promise you that."

Something in my gut believes her. But, how does she know how precious that stone is to us?

"I'm really sorry about all of it," she sighs. "It's not intentional and is certainly not personal. I have absolutely nothing against the trealfurs. In fact, when I was a little girl, I had a couple of little playmates who were trealfurs."

I try to picture this massive creature playing hide-and-seek or tag with a smattering of itty bitty trealfurs. The visual almost makes me laugh.

"I don't think it'll be a problem anymore though," the dragon assures us. "My cold's feeling much better now."

The drip of the nose goop runs down my forehead. Seems like she still has a cold to me.

She gives a giant sniff, then without warning, her neck starts flopping around, looking like the blade of grass we saw yesterday in the sky. Oh no!

"Watch out!" the dreki yells between gasps.

Judder scrambles out of the rocking chair and darts with Aspen and me out the cave's opening. The dreki turns her head away from the interior of her cave just in time, then lurches forward and lets out an ear-shattering sneeze followed by a spray of flames. Fire shoots out the entrance of her home, singeing the edges of her cave even more.

"Whoa," Aspen whispers.

I look at him with wide eyes. Whoa is right.

CHAPTER TWENTY-FIVE

Thank goodness none of us were hurt. That doesn't mean we're not shaken up, though. I've never seen anything like that. Well, I guess that's not entirely true. I did see the dreki do that exact same thing just yesterday, but she was much farther away from me. And, it was dark. Seeing it up close enough to feel the heat? Terrifying.

"I'm so sorry," the dreki calls from inside. We all step back into the cave, but stay very close to the entrance, just in case.

The dragon's eyes fill with tears again. "I'm so, so sorry," she says.

"There, there," I say again, only this time I don't dare get near enough to touch the dragon. "We get it. You're not doing these things on purpose. You're a kind dragon, not a monster like everyone thinks you are."

She shudders at my comment. Oops. Probably not the smartest choice of words. How can I make this dragon feel like we see her as nice, instead of as a monster?

"Hey." It suddenly occurs to me we don't even know what to call her. "What's your name anyway?"

The dreki sniffs and dabs a claw to her eye. "It's Talia," she says. "Talia Scalester."

Talia. "What a pretty name," I offer. I mean it, too.

"Very nice to meet you, Talia," I say. "I'm Tinsey Clover. This is my brother, Aspen, and this is Judder."

"Very nice to meet you all." Talia gives a half smile. I feel more connected to her already.

We're all doing a great job of ignoring the fact that she just nearly burned all our heads off. I look to the freshly singed perimeter of her front entrance. Too bad about that. It makes her home look way less cozy. Less clean.

That's it!

"We can help you clean up those burn marks!" I cheer. "We'll make your cave entrance look as good as new."

Aspen and Judder look at me confused. I wink at them and snap my fingers once. Twice. Three times. A wooden bucket full of goopy mud, a hallow basin of water, and a handful of round sponges appear out of thin air. Talia gasps. The mud lifts off the ground and slops itself all over the burn marks, then the basin comes in and soaks the glop till it forms a paste. Finally, the sponges float up and rub themselves back and forth against the wall. Sure enough, when the cleaning tools disappear, Talia's front entrance is sparkling and looks dazzling. Almost like new. Almost. Talia laughs.

"That was incredible!" She claps her hands together. "Simply amazing."

She wedges herself into her giant rocking chair and visibly relaxes.

I try to stay standing on my wobbly legs, but I topple over instead.

"Oh my!" Talia gasps. "Are you okay?"

"She's still working on controlling her strength after using her magic," Aspen says, kneeling next to me and feeling my forehead.

"Lavender," Talia says more to herself than to us.

"What?" I look up at her.

"Nothing," she says, looking embarrassed for her outburst. "It's just…doesn't lavender help trealfurs regain their energy?"

"It does!" Aspen cheers.

"There's some in the kitchen there," she points with her chin.

Aspen stands up and scampers off to find the herb.

"But, how do you know about that?" I ask the dreki.

She looks down sheepishly as Aspen runs back over to me and hands me a handful of lavender. I eat a nibble, then push the rest down into my shirt to save for later.

"It's not important," she says quietly. "I just had a friend once who taught me that. Anyway," she snaps her head back up and presses a smile to her lips. "Thank you for coming to find me. I haven't felt this happy in a very long time. At least, not since Mom and Dad passed away." She pauses for a second. "It's awfully lonely up here on the mountain all by myself."

I can't help the smile that spreads across my face. It feels really, really good to be here. I've done it! I've cleared up the misunderstanding. I knew the Bungaborg Dreki wasn't bad. I just knew it!

The joy is short-lived, though. The clicking of sharp animal nails on the rocks outside Talia's cave fills my ears. Faint at first, but it picks up in volume rather quickly. I look to Aspen, who looks back at me with panic in his eyes.

"Tins," he says very cautiously. "There's something I didn't tell you."

"What?" I manage to squeak.

"Remember how Sky told me last night how you saw the Bungaborg Dreki?"

I nod.

"Well, after he left, I figured I should tell someone else about it, just in case."

Oh no.

"So," he continues in barely more than a whisper, "I snuck out and told Uncle Vondur."

"You what?!"

I can't believe what I'm hearing. Aspen told the king of the trealfurs about Talia setting fire to Snugglepunk? I guess I can't really blame him—it probably was the right thing to do. But still! He could have at least waited until I did my sneaking to learn the truth about the Bungaborg Dreki.

"So…" I don't dare finish my thought.

Aspen nods, reading my mind. "He told me he'd get to the bottom of it in his own way."

We both look outside. The stampede producing the clicking sound is fully visible now. Sure enough, Uncle Vondur's leading the charge, bolting forward on top of a very angry looking mink. Behind him, an entire army of trealfurs atop their own animals follows closely, each one holding a bow in one hand, and a quiver of arrows draped across his or her shoulder.

CHAPTER TWENTY-SIX

"Uncle Vondur!" I scream, standing right in the entranceway. "Uncle Vondur, stop!"

He doesn't hear me. Or maybe he does. Either way, he keeps barreling forward, straight toward Talia's home. Two hundred paces. One-sixty. Ninety.

"Hide!" I turn around and screech at Talia.

Her almond eyes widen with fear and she gives me a helpless look. What do I expect her to do? When you're the biggest thing in the Bungaborg Forest, there aren't many hiding options. I recognize all the trealfurs. They're some of King Vondur's council people. Most of the same ones I saw sitting knee to knee for Uncle's emergency meeting. Back when I grew into my power. Was that really only yesterday? I look at each of their faces, afraid of who I might see. And then, my fears come true. I gasp.

Dad! He looks just as mad as the rest of them.

"Daddy!" I scream as he closes in on Talia's cave with the army. "Daddy, stop! She's not mean. She's a nice dreki."

Dad sees me and his eyes shift from anger to shock.

"Tinsey!" He yells as he keeps riding forward. "What are you doing here?"

Before I can give any sort of explanation, Uncle Vondur's voice booms.

"Ready!" the king calls out.

Everyone stops their animals right outside the cave entrance and takes a hold of their bows.

"Go home!" Dad demands, lifting his own bow and hardening his face again. "It's not safe here." Then, he looks away from me to follow Uncle Vondur's command instead of his daughter's plea.

"Aim!" Uncle Vondur says.

Each trealfur reaches into his or her quiver and pulls out an arrow. Every arrow is attached to a long lasso of vines. They're all pointed straight toward Talia.

"FIRE!"

A string of vines shoots behind each arrow, flying through Talia's cave and wrapping around her to form a thick net that pins her arms, her legs, and her tail against the rocking chair. She struggles against the vines, but together they're too strong, even for the Bungaborg Dreki. She's trapped.

"That was easier than I thought," Uncle Vondur smirks. "I guess you're not as tough as everyone says you are, you ugly beast!"

"It's nice to see you again, too, Vondur," Talia says gently.

What? My uncle's encountered the Bungaborg Dreki before? When?

Uncle Vondur's face tightens. I can't quite tell what emotion he's feeling, but he hesitates for a split second before scowling again.

"Let this be a lesson to you, you brute!" Uncle Vondur continues. "You have no right gallivanting through the faery ring. You know that's true. And, in case you don't get the picture, let me assure you that we've set up our defenses back in Snugglepunk. If you dare set foot—or rather, wing—anywhere near our town again, I can promise you we will not be so kind next time."

With that, he throws out a sharp whistle, and all the trealfurs' animals retreat back outside.

"Talia's not a monster!" I scream. It's a truth that needs to be said. "We've been taught our entire lives to believe that drekis are bad, but guess what? It's not true. Everything you've taught us is all a lie! Did you know trolls don't even eat trealfurs? They're bugatarians!"

"Enough," Uncle Vondur warns me.

But I'm far too riled up to stop.

"Why are we still acting this way?" I keep pushing. "Keeping us separate from the rest of the forest and teaching kids like me that everyone else around us is bad? It's barbaric! It's not true! We can be different. We should be different. Think of how great we could be if we work together instead of viewing everyone else as our enemies. We could do amazing things!"

Uncle Vondur isn't hearing a word I say, which is really too bad because it's a pretty sweet speech if you ask me. On the contrary, my comments only seem to make him angrier.

"Tinsey," Dad whispers from behind Uncle. "Stop it," he looks like he knows this will only end badly.

I hear something inside the cave. A short, gasping breath. It's Talia. I look back through the entrance to see her neck wobbling back and forth again. Oh no. Oh no!!

She sneezes and a blast of flames shoots out of her mouth, through the cave opening, right past my left shoulder—which is definitely a little too close for comfort, and straight toward the army of trealfurs. All of the animals freak out. Most of them even buck their riders off, dashing off and disappearing into the mountain fog. Even Uncle Vondur's mink leaves him breathless on the ground. The king stands up, looking more livid than ever. I half expect fire to shoot out of his face, too, he looks that furious.

"That monster is evil!" he yells, pointing at Talia. "We tried to play nice, but you've proven you can't appreciate that. And so, you leave us no choice."

He raises a hand over his head, then drops it down and yells, "ATTACK!!!"

CHAPTER TWENTY-SEVEN

The entire army of trealfurs, including Dad, charges into Talia's cave on foot. They jump onto the trapped dragon, some focusing on her feet and ankles and others climbing up her massive body to her chest and even her face. A few trealfurs shoot another round of arrows at Talia's snout, wrapping around her jaw and chin and forcing her mouth shut. They hit and pull and kick and bite, and tiny welts start popping up all over Talia's skin. She's trying her best to defend herself using the limited movement she has. There's no ignoring the pool of tears filling up in each of her kind eyes. I can't stop the tears from pooling in my own eyes, too.

Judder looks to Aspen, who looks to me. How in the world are we supposed to help our new friend? With Judder's size, he could surely counterattack and swipe some of the trealfurs away from Talia. But, that doesn't feel right because even though they're not behaving very civilly right now, they're still my people.

YEEEEEEAAAAARRRRP! The sound echoes through the cave.

My heart leaps in my chest. Sky! I turn toward the cave's entrance to see the gray fur ball racing toward Talia. He runs straight toward the dragon and starts gnawing away at the vines wrapped around her foot. While his efforts are totally valiant, he's hardly making a dent. These vines are far too strong for a little bunny's teeth. Aspen pinches his eyebrows together in thought, then runs to the front entrance of the castle and clicks out a few commands. The mink Uncle Vondur was riding on timidly approaches my brother. I can't blame the thing. It almost just got blasted away in flames. Aspen strokes its head and speaks softly to the creature. The mink visibly calms down and nods toward my brother, then scampers away. In no time, all the animals the trealfur army used to ride to Dreki Mountain stampede into the house and join Sky in gnawing away at the snare. Judder joins in, using his fingernail as a saw.

Okay, it's my turn. I close my eyes and imagine something—anything that my powers could produce to help out in this situation. A broom? No, clearly not. A rag? That definitely wouldn't do any good. Absolutely nothing comes to mind. I can't think of a single cleaning product strong enough to break through these ropes. My power is useless in this situation. And then, a different idea pops into my head. A crazy one, but crazy might just be what we need right now.

My eyes scan the space and I notice the knitting needles Judder dropped right next to a smaller, much sharper, smaller sewing needle. Does Talia cross-stitch, too?

Focus, Tinsey, I scold myself.

I look back at the knitting needles. They're positioned one on top of the other in an X formation. Perfect! I run toward the wooden spears, then lay on my belly and place my cheek on the cold ground. I squint one eye to get my calculations right. When I'm certain of my math, I use all my strength to push the top needle ever so slightly to the left, then climb onto one end of it, making the top needle fall to the ground with my weight, like a seesaw.

"Judder!" I call.

When he looks up, I wave him over to me.

"Jump on the other side!" I shout.

He nods and runs toward me, leaving the vines he's working on. I take a good look at his body and really hope I guessed his weight correctly. If he weighs the two hundred pounds I assume he does, that means his force will be strong enough to launch me into a thirty-degree arc. Here's to hoping. Judder runs over, jumps and lands on the pointy end of the needle, forcing that side down and my side upward. I fly through the air at the perfect angle, landing right where I expected just below Talia's ear. Yes!

I scramble behind one of her purple scales, where I'm hidden from all the trealfurs attacking her front side and take a deep breath.

"Talia," I say loudly into her ear. "I've never been a great trealfur. I can't sing to save my life.

But, I'm great with numbers. More often than not, I even daydream in numbers. Sometimes, I feel like it's a pointless activity, but other times, I wonder if there's lots of power in that type of thing. Maybe you could try it and hope it's the powerful kind?"

She gives a tiny nod.

"Great," I say. "Now, close your eyes and picture yourself in this exact same situation. Only, instead of being completely trapped and helpless, you're laughing. Laughing because it's ridiculous that these tiny people who are one sixtieth of your size think they can hold you down. You! The strongest creature in the entire forest. The Bungaborg Dreki."

I notice a teensy tiny smile appear under her snout. Perfect.

"Now, picture flexing your arm and pulling it off the chair. C'mon, picture it. I bet you could easily lift five hundred pounds. These vines couldn't weight more than five pounds. One hundred times lighter. Don't let your mind fool you into thinking you're defeated or trapped. You're definitely strong enough, Talia!"

"But, nobody wants me here. I should just let them win." She sighs.

"That is so not true!" I exclaim. "We want you here! We need you here. You're strong enough Talia. Do it for all of us. Do it for you!"

At my words, her arm actually flexes in real life and pulls off the chair. Thanks to the help of Judder and all of Aspen's animals, the ropes around one arm snap and a couple of the trealfurs lose their balance and fall off.

"GREAT!" I cheer into her ear. "Now, the other arm. You can do it, Talia! I know you can!"

She raises her other arm. A couple of the vines easily snap on that side. Yes! She follows that up by shaking her neck free. Then, she shimmies her shoulders. If I didn't know better, I'd say she actually looks like she's having a bit of fun! Trealfurs are falling off her one by one, dropping back to the ground, then scrambling to safety as the dreki becomes less and less restricted. At last, Talia kicks the final few vines off her feet and stands up. She's free! She shakes the remaining trealfurs off of her, including Uncle Vondur.

"Come on!" I scream down to Aspen and Judder, who respond by climbing up and joining me on her back.

Talia strides outside of her cave. She spreads her humongous wings, which are even more impressive than I originally thought, and flaps them proudly. At the last minute, Sky the bunny spy runs out of the cave and hops onto the dragon's back behind me. I smile and give his fuzzy head a pat. He just stares back at me with his black, beady eyes.

We lift off the ground, riding on the majestic dragon's back, and soar off Dreki Mountain, leaving it all behind.

CHAPTER TWENTY-EIGHT

If you've ever wondered what it's like to ride on a dreki's back, I can tell you it's the most exhilarating experience you'll ever have. I highly recommend it. Talia flies so smoothly, it almost feels like we're not moving at all. Of course, we are moving, and very quickly at that. I watch as the entire forest spreads out below us. It looks like a giant quilt from up here, with sections of dark green followed by chunks of light green, a bunch of browns, and even some blues that must be little bodies of water. The air up here is crisp and clear. It smells like freedom. I close my eyes and let the wind whip through my shaggy hair, not caring one bit as the purple strands fly wildly into my face. Let them feel the freedom, too.

I'm not sure where we're going, but I have a pretty

good idea. Talia confirms my hunch by taking a sharp left at just the right spot. The engi comes into view, then the tall wall of Snugglepunk's vines peek out from one edge. We're going home.

That's all well and good for me and Aspen, and even Judder will have an easy time finding his way back to Rumplelawn. What about Talia, though? What will she do? I'm sure Uncle Vondur's furious after his failed plan. He'll only build up an even stronger army and keep trying until he succeeds. And suddenly, I remember. Uncle Vondur!

I look behind us, fearing the worst, and sure enough, it exists. Uncle Vondur can fly. What in the world is he thinking? I mean, I know Talia's a gentle dreki and all, but she is still an enormous dragon. One that's been wronged. It was one thing when the king had a whole army backing him up, but now he's chasing her on his own? I'm pretty certain even the kindest creatures will defend themselves when provoked. I'm not sure who I'm more worried about right now, Talia or Uncle Vondur. Why oh why can Uncle Vondur fly?

I snap my fingers over and over again. Everything

from brooms to mops to buckets fall from the sky toward my uncle. He spins and dips, dodging everything I throw at him. At least it slows him down a little bit. I take a nibble of the lavender tucked inside my shirt to keep my strength. Uncle Vondur changes his course, turning back toward Dreki Mountain and retreating out of sight. I sigh in relief. But, I'm sure he's not giving up. If anything, he's probably got a plan of attack up his sleeve. At least his retreat buys us some time, though. But, it still doesn't answer the question: Where will Talia go? I certainly can't hide her in Snugglepunk, and I'm betting the trolls in Rumplelawn won't be so keen on sharing their space with what they think is an evil dragon. But, she's not evil! A new resolve creeps into my whole body. It's time to change the way the forest sees this beautiful creature.

"She'll be safe in the engi for at least a little while," I call back to Aspen and Judder, even though they haven't heard any part of the conversation going on inside my head.

"What are you talking about?" Aspen asks, shaking his head.

I sigh. He's my brother, isn't he supposed to be able to read my mind?

"We've got to tell Mom about Talia," I say. "And Judder, you need to tell your mom."

Aspen and Judder both look beyond confused.

"They're our best bets. If we can at least get them onboard, maybe they can help us defend her. I mean, Mom is the sister of the King, after all. If she believes in Talia, don't you think that could influence quite a few people?"

"But, how da you's know they won't freak out an' start attackin' Talia, too?" Judder asks.

Fair question.

"Because Mom will listen to us," I say. I really believe it. "She trusts us."

Aspen nods. He feels it, too.

"And Judder," I call back. "I've only met your mom once, but I can tell she'll listen to you, too. She loves you more than the entire world."

Judder blushes and tries to hide his smile, but there's no denying it: he's a mama's boy through and through.

CHAPTER TWENTY-NINE

We land in the engi and doubt seeps into my body. I mean, I knew the meadow was wide-open, but it didn't really matter much before. Now that we're trying to protect a shimmering dragon the size of a small mountain, I'm realizing the wide-open space maybe wasn't our best choice for a hiding spot.

"I should go back to my volcano," Talia says firmly. "We can all just go back to the way things were."

"No!" I say quickly. "At least, not yet. It's time to change a few things around here."

I try throwing some tall weeds over her, but what's tall for me is like an ant compared to her. There's no time for a plan B, though. I cross all my fingers and even my toes and hope that'll give us enough luck for this to work.

"I'll stay and keep watch," Aspen says.

I give him a big thumbs up and my heart pounds with love. My brother is seriously the coolest person in the entire world.

"See's ya's back heres soon!" Judder's voice trails off as he shuffles toward Rumplelawn.

"Okay," I say to Aspen. "I'll go as fast as I can. If Uncle Vondur shows up…"

I stop mid-sentence, because I have absolutely no idea what Aspen should do if our uncle shows up. Try to fight him off? Keep Talia from attacking him?

"I'll take care of it, Tins."

I smile.

"Oh, and here," he says. "Take this." He whistles and a stunning, silver fox speeds toward us. Aspen pats the animal's back once it stops. "It'll get you there much quicker."

I climb on and the thing takes off, darting through the engi so quickly, my eyes start to water. Sky runs behind us, easily keeping up. We break through the vines of Snugglepunk and I'm shocked by how good it feels to be back here! For once, I appreciate all the trees. They somehow seem less dull than before. More comforting. As we get closer to my cave, I even spot Fred the mouse nestled by his favorite bush. Talk about a welcome sight!

"Hey, Fred!" I call out, although I don't have time to stop and chat. "Great to see you, buddy!"

He lifts his tiny nose in response. We ride on till we reach the entrance to my family cave. I hop off my ride and give it a quick hug to say thanks.

"Mom?" I call as I step through the opening.

No answer.

"Mom?" I try again.

I hear something in the back room. What is that? Is Mom crying? I run into our cave toward the sound.

"Mom, are you okay?" I ask when I see her sitting cross-legged on the ground with her back to me.

She startles at my voice, then turns around and rises to her feet.

"Oh, Tinsey!" she cries, throwing her arms around me. "Oh, Tinsey, I've been so worried about you! About all of you!"

It suddenly occurs to me that my mom was probably tasked with staying inside Snugglepunk as acting heir while the king took the rest of his council to Dreki Mountain. Which means she's been sitting here all day by herself without knowing where her children were, and whether or not her husband had been burned by a dragon.

"I'm okay, Mom."

I'm not quite sure how to say the next part, though. The part where I need to convince her to side with the Bungaborg Dreki. I tack on my most charming smile. The one that used to always work when I was little and wanted an extra helping of berry stew after dinner.

"Um, Mom?" I bat my eyes just as an extra touch.

She pulls back and looks at me with concern in her eyes. Where do I even start?

"You know the Bungaborg Dreki?"

Mom nods slowly. Of course she knows the Bungaborg Dreki. I bet it's been the only thing she's thought about today.

"Well, she needs your help. Our help."

"What do you mean?" Mom asks with a thick layer of caution in her voice.

Fair enough. I wasn't expecting her to just agree on the spot.

"So…err…I…had this idea that maybe the dragon wasn't as awful as everyone says. You know, like maybe she's actually nice. I mean, why couldn't she be, right?"

Mom doesn't answer. She doesn't do anything at all. She just stares at me. So, I go on.

"Anyway, I had that thought yesterday when I saw the dragon…" I stop myself. I wasn't planning on admitting I snuck out of Snugglepunk yesterday, but I guess there's no avoiding it. It's bound to come out at some point or another. "…when I snuck out into the engi yesterday."

Mom nods once. The look in her eyes tells me she already knew I'd done that. Of course she does. Moms know everything.

"Well," I continue, "I saw the dragon take your family's stone, and I couldn't just let that happen. So, I went to the volcano and met her. And, you know what? She's not mean at all. I know it sounds crazy, but I swear it's true. In fact, I think you'd really like her."

Mom's eyes widen. Here it comes. I brace myself for my punishment.

When she speaks, her voice isn't stern, though. It's filled with surprise. "You met Talia?" she asks.

My jaw drops. How does she know Talia's name?

"Yes…" I say slowly. "Do you know Talia?"

The room starts spinning at the realization. My mom knows the Bungaborg Dreki.

CHAPTER THIRTY

"Back when I was a little girl," Mom starts her story, "way before I met your dad and definitely before my older brother, your Uncle Vondur, became king, my grandpa ruled Snugglepunk. He was a gentle trealfur and a great leader. Everyone loved him. Of course, it's easy to love your king when everything's peaceful all around you. The Bungaborg Forest was open to everyone. I don't remember much about it, but I do remember playing in the engi with yulemen, blomalfurs, and trolls alike. We always had so much fun together. Our parents didn't mind one bit. Of course they didn't. There was no hatred in Bungaborg yet. Only acceptance.

"That included everyone. Even the Bungaborg Drekis. There was a whole family of them back then: a grandma, a mom and dad, and a little girl about my age. Her name was Talia."

I can't hide the surprise that leaps onto my face. When Talia was talking about playing with the trealfurs when she was little, was she referring to my mom?

"We loved playing with her," Mom goes on. "After all, who wouldn't like to have a gargantuan friend who can fly you around on her back?"

Good point.

"But then, Grandfather passed away. My father took over as ruler, and had very sour opinions about the huldufolk outside of Snugglepunk. To be honest, I was far too young to understand the politics of it all, but the one thing I did know was that my friendships were being taken away from me one by one. The blomalfurs stopped coming to play, then the trolls and yulemen, then the sprites. And finally, Talia. I'll never forget the day I heard Father having that heated argument with the adult drekis. He was so livid. He swore he'd kill each and every one of them if he ever saw them again..." Her voice trails off.

"Did he…" I start to ask, but can't stand to finish my question.

Mom nods.

"He ended up killing both Talia's parents. After that, my father declared that no trealfurs were allowed to leave Snugglepunk ever again. So, that was that. Stories—lies really—started spreading to explain why we couldn't play with all our friends, like the trolls anymore. 'Because they eat trealfurs,' the adults would say. After seeing what my father did to the drekis, no one dared challenge him.

"But, it didn't used to be like that. We used to have so much fun together. Even my brother, your Uncle Vondur, would play with the drekis. He loved them. At least, until Father convinced him they were evil. Sad how quickly a person can change, isn't it?"

Wait, what?! Uncle Vondur used to play with Talia, too? The thought makes me sick to my stomach. I try to picture him as a little boy, laughing and running around with the dragon, but it's impossible to imagine. The only picture that keeps coming to mind is Uncle Vondur today, beating on poor Talia's skin with that nasty grin on his face.

"Was it hard to watch your brother and your husband go off today to fight her?" I ask, already knowing the answer.

She nods. "I know she's not mean. At least she didn't used to be. Crazy what growing up can do to a person, though."

She pauses and her eyes drift away from me for a second. I wonder if she's thinking about Uncle Vondur.

"He's just following in Father's footsteps," Mom says, like she knows I'm thinking about her big brother. "It's not a rare thing to see."

I don't like that she's trying to defend my uncle. I snap her attention back to the issue at hand.

"Talia's not mean," I insist. "She's really, really nice. You'll see. You would have cried today if you'd seen the pain in her eyes when they were beating her."

Mom shoots her glance back at me.

"What did they do to her?" she asks with a tremble in her voice.

"Don't worry, we helped save her, Mom! But, she needs your help, too. She's in the engi right now waiting for us. Aspen's watching over her."

"Aspen's in on all this, too?"

Oops. I hope I didn't just get my brother into trouble. This whole thing was my idea, he was just trying to keep me safe.

Mom's face tells me she's processing all of this. I can't blame her. I don't dare say anything else to her. She already has enough reasons to ground me for life; I don't need to give her more. I do kinda want to hurry things along a bit, though. Who knows what's going on with Talia and Uncle Vondur right now. I wish Mom would at least say something, even if it is to yell at me.

When Mom finally does speak, it's not to ground me.

In a gentle, but strong tone, she simply says, "Tinsey, take me to her."

CHAPTER THIRTY-ONE

The fox is still waiting for me outside our cave when we emerge, but Sky's nowhere to be seen. I twist my mouth in guilt. I guess I didn't actually think Mom would come with me, otherwise I would've asked Aspen for a bigger animal. Mom doesn't miss a beat, though.

"Come on, sweetheart," she says, leading the way toward the fox. "You can sit on my lap."

I do as she says, and in no time, we're racing back through Snugglepunk toward the opening in the vines. Mom knows the way perfectly. Of course she does. She spent her childhood making this same trek to the engi all the time.

When we get through the clearing, we see Talia immediately. I'm embarrassed all over again for my lousy idea of trying to hide her in the engi. Luckily,

Uncle Vondur isn't anywhere to be seen. Yet. Aspen's still standing right by Talia's side. He lights up when he sees us.

"Hey, sweetheart," Mom says to my brother. "Hi, Talia," she says much more timidly to the dragon.

Talia looks at her confused. I don't blame her. I bet Mom looks way different than she did back then.

"It's Jade," Mom says, placing her hand on her chest. "Jade Clover."

Talia's eyes get all sorts of wide and she lets out a small gasp.

"Jade?!" She repeats the name.

Mom nods. "It's really good to see you, Talia."

"Wow," Talia still looks completely shocked. "Great to see you too, Jade. Can you believe so much time has passed?"

"Yeah," Mom sighs. "And to think it was right here in this meadow where we used to have so much fun together. How did the forest come to this?" She looks sad. Like, really sad.

Talia nods solemnly. I lower my head and look

at the ground for a second because it feels like a moment that's meant for just Mom and her long-lost friend. Someone else bursts into their bubble anyway, though.

"Hey, guys!" Judder's back, and he's not alone. "Dis is me's mom, Slimetta."

"So nice ta meet's you's all," Slimetta waves.

She catches my eye and blushes through her cookie dough cheeks.

"Sorry fer all dat mess back at da house earlier's."

I shrug like it's no big deal, even though she was this close to smashing my brother with a giant rock. Hopefully we're all on the same team now. That's what matters.

"Slimetta?" Mom asks with a fair amount of surprise attached. "Slimetta Sludge?"

"Dat's me's," Judder's mom says, raising an eyebrow toward Mom.

"Slimetta," Mom says again. "It's me, Jade Clover!"

"Jade Clover?!" Slimmer gasps. "Jade Clover who's used ta climb all da ways up ta da tips of da trees an' den screech at da tops of her lungs with her hideous-soundin' voice pretendin' you's was a bird? You's always had da worst singin' voice of 'em all!"

Talia laughs like she remembers that moment, too. Mom's cheeks redden and she looks toward me and Aspen. My mom was a bad singer, too? Judder's mom slaps her hand over her mouth like she's just spilled some big secret.

"Ya didn't hear's dat frum me's, kids. Yer mom's just liked ta have fun and be her own person, dat's all. Always marchin' ta da beat of her own drum an' proud of it. Use ta drive her parents crazy." She laughs at the memory and Mom just blushes more.

I, on the other hand, beam with pride. So that's where I get my little quirks from. How come she never told me all that stuff before? And then I remember: Uncle Vondur. Did he once use his imagination, too?

As if the simple mention of his name was all it took, Uncle Vondur comes flying into view, interrupting the little reunion going on here. He's zooming straight toward Talia. Beneath him on the ground, his army of trealfurs is charging toward the dragon, too. Just as I thought, Uncle Vondur has a plan. And they all look mad. Really mad.

CHAPTER THIRTY-TWO

Uncle Vondur screams to his army as he pierces through the perfectly blue sky. They all pick up speed.

"It's time to end this, Dreki!" He cries, pointing something straight toward Talia's heart.

I squint to get a closer look. It's the little sewing needle that was sitting next to Talia's knitting needles! I'm not sure what kind of harm my uncle thinks he can do with a two-foot long needle. It'd hardly even pierce through Talia's skin I bet! But then, I notice something attached to the tip of the needle. What is it? I squint my eyes to see better. It looks like a tiny half-moon. And, it's purple. Oh no! It's one of those berries Judder stopped me from eating back in the forest. It's pure poison!

I jump in front of Talia to protect her, but very

quickly remember that I only come up to her big toe. I couldn't take the hit even if I wanted to.

"Talia, fly away!" I scream.

She spreads her wings and lifts up into the blue sky, pointing in the direction of Dreki Mountain. But then, she turns. What is she doing?

"Leave!" I scream up to her.

I'm sure she doesn't hear me. She looks different somehow. Angry.

"You've kept my friends from me for all these years," she growls at Uncle Vondur. "How dare you!"

Her words don't seem to matter at all to him. He's still flying at full speed, poisoned needle at the ready, straight toward the dreki's chest. She jets toward him ten times faster. Each of the trealfur soldiers on the ground aims his or her bow and arrow at Talia.

"No!" I shriek.

I close my eyes and brace myself for whatever sound a trealfur smashing into a dreki might make, but that doesn't happen. Instead, I hear the voice of my mom, and she's singing a very high-pitched lullaby. I open my eyes, totally confused. This is no time for songs! But, apparently it is, because Uncle Vondur and Talia aren't closing in on each other anymore. Instead, they're both floating in midair, like they've been momentarily frozen.

That's right! It's Mom's magical power! The ability to sing above a certain pitch and make the whole forest stop to listen, if only for a second. How lucky is that? The part that isn't so lucky, however, is that Uncle Vondur and Talia aren't the only ones who are frozen. None of us can move, not even me. When Mom finishes her verse, Uncle Vondur and Talia shake back to life, but they don't have any momentum anymore and both drop straight down to the ground. The king's makeshift weapon clatters next to him, which gives Talia just enough time to spread her incredible wings and take off back into the sky. More arrows shoot upward toward her, all of them falling short. Uncle Vondur stands up and shakes himself off, picks up the needle, and jumps back into flight as well.

Uncle Vondur may be tiny, but he's surprisingly fast. He sneaks up right behind the dragon and latches himself onto her hind leg.

"Talia!" I scream. "Behind you!"

But, it's too late. My voice gets lost in a sudden and extremely strong gust of wind.

Wind? But, the skies are perfectly clear. This isn't like your typical windy day wind, either. It feels more like a tornado, pushing the tall grasses around and even breaking off some branches from the swaying trees around the engi's perimeter. My hair flies around my head in every which direction. Even Aspen's normally perfect hair is ruffled up a bit. If we weren't in the middle of such a dire situation, I'd mention it just to rub it in. But there's no time to tease anyone about anything. I'm too worried I'm going to be lifted off the ground any second. I grab onto a tall blade of grass with my entire body, just for security.

A handful of the trealfur army falls over, and it looks like Uncle Vondur's barely hanging on, too. Sure, he's still gripping onto Talia, but it appears to be getting harder and harder for him. His fingers start sliding down her scales. His other hand refuses to let go of the needle. In the end, it's a lost cause. His hand loses its hold on the dragon and he goes spinning out of control in another swirl of wind. We all watch his little body as it flips and cartwheels, like it's dancing on the air. I even start laughing, although that's probably not the right thing to be doing right now. I can't help it, though. He looks so ridiculous!

I still can't figure out where this wind is coming from. I can't remember ever feeling anything like this. I look to Mom for an answer. She's got this giant grin on her face, like she knows exactly what's going on.

"Look," she says, pointing to the horizon with her chin.

Sure enough, I see a tiny black dot coming in from behind the trealfur army. It's growing bigger and bigger until it's close enough for me to see it clearly.

Running toward us in the engi is Dad.

CHAPTER THIRTY-THREE

Of course! Dad's magical power is the ability to cause massive windstorms! But, I thought for sure he was on Uncle Vondur's side? He definitely looked pretty angry at Talia back on Dreki Mountain. What changed his mind?

"Hey honey!" Dad pants as he gets close enough to hear us. "Thought I might see you here."

Mom grins and throws her arms around him. The wind dies down all around us. Whatever trealfur soldiers who are still upright tumble over from the surprise of the sudden calm.

"Of course I'd be here. You know, our daughter is quite persuasive." She looks at me and winks.

"I couldn't agree more," Dad laughs, then pulls me into their hug with them.

"Hey," Aspen calls from behind us.

Dad rolls his eyes. "Okay, okay. You can be part of our family hug too, son."

"No," Aspen says. "I mean, thanks and all, but LOOK!"

We all turn just in time to see Uncle Vondur, who's gained full control now that there's no wind. He's flying straight toward Talia!

"NO!" I cry, but it's no use. It's too late.

Uncle Vondur stabs Talia with her own sewing needle right at the base of her left wing. She lurches backward and screeches. She continues to fly, but her left wing starts looking more and more floppy. The dreki's whole body tilts with the failing limb, then starts into a free fall. Trealfurs scatter everywhere. Uncle Vondur stays afloat in the air, a nasty grin on his face. Out of the blue, another sound fills my ears. One that seems to make my heart stop beating.

SCREECH!

It's the gyrfalcon! The same one that tried to carry me away yesterday, I'm sure of it. The brown bird quickly comes into view and my mind jumps into action. The predator's flying in fast, at about a fifteen-degree angle from the left. If it stays on course, it'll run right into Uncle Vondur.

"Uncle Vondur!" I scream. "Move!"

Even though he isn't being the kindest person at the moment, I still don't want to see the king of the trealfurs get hurt. He looks straight down at me. His lips curl up and he shakes his head.

"Nobody tells the king what to do, my dear," he snarls, then spits at me. Yes! A spray of my uncle's spit seriously lands on top of my head, right where Talia's runny snot is now all crusty.

Welp, I tried to warm him.

The falcon doesn't waste any time. It stays on its fifteen-degree angle and dives straight toward my uncle. Before King Vondur can even see what's going on, the bird snatches him up in its rough talons. I try not to let it get to me. I tell myself to be okay with that falcon taking my uncle away to feed its babies. After all, he deserves that, right? But, as hard as I try, I just can't let it happen.

I look down and find a small pebble, the size of a berry if even that. I grab Dad's bow, which is draped over his right shoulder, then position the rock and make some quick calculations. Fifteen feet off the ground. Thirty degrees to my left. No wind. I pull the bow back, then release it and watch the pebble fly. It hits the bird directly on its beak. Perfect shot! The falcon shrieks in surprise, then opens its talons and lets my uncle drop. Down, down, down. *Thunk.* He lands in a bush. A very healthy thistle bush with lots of purple burrs. Serves him right.

I walk over to the bush and reach out my hand to help him up.

"Why are you doing this?" he asks, a thistle poking right out of the top of his hairline. "Why didn't you let that falcon kill me?"

"Because, even though I don't agree with a single thing you do," I say, "you're still my family."

He looks at my outstretched hand for a few seconds, like he's debating what to do. Finally, he reaches out and takes a hold of me. I help him stand up. He grimaces when he puts weight on his left leg. It's clear he hurt it pretty badly. I support him as he limps and we make our way together back toward Mom and Dad. Judder and his mom don't say a word.

"Hey!" one of the trealfur soldiers calls, seemingly noticing the two trolls for the first time. "Why aren't they eating us?"

"Yeah!" another one shouts. "They don't seem mean at all. Neither does that dreki. What's that all about?"

"And the engi is actually pretty nice. The whole forest is!" a third one says.

The whole army nods their agreement. They all look toward their King, who sinks down and tries to hide behind Mom.

"Why would you deny us the freedom to come out here?" one asks. "Why have you been lying to us?"

They start talking over each other, like they did back at the council meeting yesterday.

"Silence, everyone!" Uncle Vondur cries, limping out from behind Mom.

He looks ridiculous with burrs sticking out in all different directions. For the first time ever, not a single trealfur obeys his command. If anything, they just get louder.

"Sorry to say it, Uncle," I shrug. "But, I think

the people have spoken. I've been to enough council meetings to know that we vote by majority." I turn to the other trealfurs. "All in favor of King Vondur handing over the crown to my mom?"

Every single elf raises his or her hand. Judder does too, although I don't think that counts. My grin spreads from cheek to cheek.

"Well, there you have it, then! All hail Queen Jade!" I cheer.

"All hail Queen Jade!" The crowd repeats.

Mom looks stunned. Dad looks thrilled. Uncle Vondur looks...well, defeated.

When the cheering dies down, I hear what could barely be called a whimper.

Talia!

CHAPTER THIRTY-FOUR

I rush over to my dragon friend, who's crumpled in a giant ball, panting heavily.

"Talia!" I cry. "Talia, are you okay?"

"Yes," she whispers weakly. "I think so. I'll be okay." Even though her voice doesn't sound very convincing, I hope she's telling the truth. "Tinsey," she says, looking into my emerald green eyes with her matching ones. "You did it. You changed the way we look at things in the forest."

"But I didn't!" I protest, crying so hard, snot shoots out my nose. I don't even care. "I ruined everything, Talia. If it wasn't for me, you wouldn't be hurt."

"You don't understand, Tinsey," she gasps from the pain. "I was hurt before I met you. My heart was hurt from loneliness. But you healed it. You brought me here. You shared your friends and your family with me. Thank you, my dear."

I nuzzle my head into her tail and sob. She'll be okay, right? Please tell me she'll be okay.

"She'll be okay," Aspen says, kneeling next to me and placing his hand on my back. "He just pierced her wing, nothing serious."

"But," I stammer, "there was poison on the tip."

Aspen's face goes pale. He stands up and tries to get me to do the same.

"No!" I shout, pushing him away. "Don't touch me! I won't leave her." I turn to the rest of the crowd. "Does anyone have anything we can clean this wound with?"

Nobody steps forward.

Wait. Clean the wound? I close my eyes and try to think. What would clean poison out of a wound?

"Witch hazel!" Mom cries out in the crowd below.

I turn to look at her.

"Witch hazel helps pull out toxins," she says.

I nod, then close my eyes again and picture a

stem of witch hazel flowers. I think of Talia and feel the warmth for her run from my heart down my arm and out my fingers. *Snap!*

Even as my knees start to get wobbly, I won't let myself quit. I rub the flowers all over Talia's wound. Once I'm through, the flowers all disappear and a large leaf floats over and flattens across the wound like a bandage. Talia gives me a feeble smile.

"Thanks," she says.

"Wait," I realize. "That's not everything."

I scoot right up to the bandage and give it a kiss.

"There. Everything heals better with a little love."

I take a bite of lavender for strength, then step down off the dreki and take my place next to Mom, who gives me a tearful hug.

"As the new queen of the trealfurs," Mom turns to the crowd and says with all the authority in the world. "I hereby declare today the Bungaborg Trealfur Day of Peace."

Sounds like a great idea to me! Except, we're only a small percentage of the trealfur community, let alone the entire huldufolk population. Who's to say the way we feel right here in this meadow is the same way everyone all across the forest will feel? I'm sure there are plenty of people who won't be so keen on just allowing the trealfurs back into their lives. Not to mention the trealfurs who won't want to open our walls.

Mom looks at me like she's reading my thoughts.

"I say we hold an emergency council," she says. "Right here, right now. To get everyone's opinion on the matter. We'll start with the trealfurs and the trolls, then move on from there. What do you say to that?"

I nod. Sounds like a good plan. No. Sounds like a great plan!

"Slimetta?" Mom calls to Judder's mom.

"Yes?"

"Would you mind announcing a troll-wide meeting in the engi for me?"

Slimetta nods, "It would be me's honor," she bows slightly, then grabs her son's hand and starts back toward the weeping willow clump.

"Wait," I call.

Slimetta and Judder both turn around.

"Talia? How are you feeling?" I ask.

She nods. "Much better now."

"Great," I say. "Do you think you could fly Judder back to Dreki Mountain? That is, if it's okay with you Ms. Slimetta?"

"Sure," Talia says. "But, why?"

"Well," I say. "I think what this emergency council meeting could really use is some good food. And, it just so turns out, I happen to know a great chef and a great garden full of veggies."

Judder beams. "Can I's, Mom?"

Slimetta smiles and nods. Judder runs over and climbs onto Talia's back, giving her bandage a kiss on the way up. Talia spreads her wings and, in a heartbeat, they're off, soaring through the air toward Dreki Mountain.

Aspen summons a couple of foxes and he and Dad ride on them back into Snugglepunk to call all the trealfurs. Mom stays with me in the engi.

"I'm really proud of you, sweetheart," she says, sitting down next to me. "You stood up for yourself. You felt an injustice in your heart and you did something about it, even when it wasn't the popular thing to do. That shows a maturity well beyond your years."

I blush.

"In fact," she continues. "As the new queen of Snugglepunk, I would be honored to have you run our first council meeting."

"Me?" I gasp.

Doesn't she remember that I was the kid who rolled through the circle and into a thistle bush at our last meeting? Doesn't she remember how I made cleaning products appear out of nowhere and disrupted everything?

"I remember," she says, and I'm suddenly freaked out by how well Mom can read my mind. "I remember how beautiful it all was because you were being you. What could possibly be better than that?"

I throw my arms around her and swear I'll never let go.

As the sun starts setting in the sky, I see Talia and Judder flying down from Dreki Mountain.

Next to Judder, there's enough food to feed the entire forest. In Talia's claw, the Snugglepunk Safety Stone glistens in the fading daylight. Talia looks to Mom, who smiles and lifts her hand up. She pinches her fingers together, then opens them up wide, making a gesture that looks like she's letting go of something. Talia smiles. She understands. She opens her talon and the blue stone drops down, smashing into pieces when it hits the ground.

I guess we won't be needing that to keep people out of Snugglepunk anymore.

The trees to the north and east of us start to shake. From the north, a slew of animals stampede into the engi, each one carrying a trealfur on its back. Leading the charge is Sky, the bunny spy, carrying one of the younger elves. Even Fred the mouse is part of the charge, running with a big grin on his face. From the east, a group of trolls all shuffle their way to us, each one looking more undercooked than the next. Every single trealfur shields his or her eyes as they enter the meadow. Just like I did the first time I came here. It occurs to me, this is the first time any of our people have been out here in years. A tingle runs up and down my spine because I know, no matter how much I flub up this council meeting, it doesn't really matter. Things are already shifting in the Bungaborg Forest. And, if you ask me, they're definitely shifting for the better.

ACKNOWLEDGEMENTS

Thanks to everyone who helped breath life into Tinsey and her adventure! From Pat Concordia, who believed in this character right from the beginning, to Brad Wilson at Yellow Bird Editors for not being afraid to offer real critiques to help bring the story to the next level. Thanks to the ever talented Kelly Angelovic for the perfect cover illustration, and to Jess Torbin for her perfect insights on how to bring this book into the world. Thanks to the agents at Andrea Brown Literary Agency for their wonderful Big Sur Writer's Workshop that connected me to some great ideas and even greater people. Thanks to Miss Annika's first grade class who were all eager listeners and helpers with my story. Thanks to my friends and family for the countless hours you spent listening to me talk over and over and over about Tinsey. Finally, an especially huge thanks to my husband, Bill, and my three daughters, Quincy, Olive, and Pearl. You're not only the best beta readers known to man, but my heart's exploding knowing you're also my biggest fans. I'm your biggest fan, too. I love you all!

Made in the USA
San Bernardino, CA
15 January 2019